This book should be returned to any branch of the
Lancashire County Library on or before the date shown

1 2· AUG 2016

2 6 AUG 2016

2 8 JAN 201

1 4 APR 201

- 4 APR 2020

- 7 JUN 2016

www.lancashire.gov.uk/libraries

LL1(A)

Lanc

301

D0551452

LOUISE'S GAMBLE

*Young widow Louise Pearlie becomes embroiled
in a perilous game of mafia bosses, Nazi spies
and banished royalty in this wartime novel
of suspense*

1942, Washington DC. Young widow Louise
Pearlie is now a chief file clerk at the legendary OSS, the precursor to the CIA, and
enjoying being an independent, working
woman despite wartime privations. But a
casual friendship struck up with Alessa di
Luca, a secretive war refugee, sucks Louise
into a dangerous game of mafia bosses, Nazi
spies, banished royalty and Sicilian aristocracy – placing not only her job, but her life,
in jeopardy...

LOUISE'S GAMBLE

Sarah R. Shaber

Severn House Large Print
London & New York

This first large print edition published 2013
in Great Britain and the USA by
SEVERN HOUSE PUBLISHERS LTD of
19 Cedar Road, Sutton, Surrey, England, SM2 5DA.
First world regular print edition published 2012 by
Severn House Publishers Ltd., London and New York.

British Library Cataloguing in Publication Data

Shaber, Sarah R. author.
  Louise's gamble. -- Large print edition. -- (A Louise
  Pearlie mystery ; 2)
  1. Pearlie, Louise (Fictitious character)--Fiction.
  2. United States. Office of Strategic Services--
  Employees--Fiction. 3. Suspense fiction. 4. Large type
  books.
  I. Title II. Series
  813.6-dc23

ISBN-13: 9780727896407

Severn House Publishers support the Forest Stewardship
Council™ [FSC™], the leading international forest certification
organisation. All our titles that are printed on FSC certified paper
carry the FSC logo.

Printed and bound in Great Britain by
T J International, Padstow, Cornwall.

*For my writing buddies: Margaret Maron,
Brenda Witchger, Katy Munger, Diane
Chamberlain, Alexandra Sokoloff and Kathy
Trocheck (Mary Kay Andrews).
I can't imagine my life without you!*

ACKNOWLEDGEMENTS

First I must thank my family for their continued support and encouragement. My husband, Steve, son Sam, and daughter Katie have endured the trials of my writing career right along with me. Katie is my official first reader. She always knows what I need to do to improve my books, and even better she's mastered how to tell me!

My writing buddies, Margaret Maron, Kathy Trochek, Brenda Witchger, Alex Sokoloff, Katy Munger, and Diane Chamberlain, to whom this book is dedicated, are irreplaceable colleagues and friends.

Many thanks to my agent, Vicky Bijur, for her professionalism, patience and friendship. And I am so fortunate that my home bookstore is Quail Ridge Books here in Raleigh.

I am grateful to Edwin Buckhalter, Rachel Simpson Hutchens, and Michelle Duff, at Severn House Publishers, for taking on my new series during such a difficult time for publishers.

7

Prolog

'Jesus, Mary and Joseph!' Turi said. *'Mia piccola sorella*! I thought I would never see you again!'

Alessa flung herself into her brother's arms, eyes streaming. Turi encircled her body in a bear hug. Just as she thought her ribs might crack he released her and held her out in front of him, taking her in from head to foot.

'When the boss man said a fine lady was asking for me, he wasn't kidding,' Turi said. 'When did you arrive?'

'Months ago,' Alessa said. 'We thought we could tolerate Mussolini until after the war, but when the Nazis built their Stuka bomber nests we left.'

Turi held up ten fingers in his boss's direction, and the man nodded his permission.

'Come,' Turi said, leading Alessa away from the clamor of the dockyards. They stepped over a coil of rope as thick as Turi's arm and stood on the landward side of a metal and tar-paper shack at the foot of a massive West Side pier. Almost every berth was

9

occupied by a cargo ship or Navy vessel. The air reeked of motor oil and creosote. Seagulls wheeled and shrieked overhead. Dozens of longshoremen, some operating tall winches or forklifts, loaded the ships with crates. As soon as trucks were emptied, new ones pulled up on the dock, piled with more crates.

'So,' Turi said, 'you didn't forget your father's *bastardo.*'

'Of course not! And Papa loved you, Turi.'

'As much as he could, I suppose.'

'He hid you in the cellar for days and then smuggled you out of Sicily and paid your fare here, didn't he?'

'Yes, little one, he did. But enough about him. Do you have any children yet?'

'We're going to wait until after the war is over.'

Turi shrugged. 'Pfft, there will always be wars,' he said. 'Me, I have four! Two boys, two girls!'

Alessa's eyes lit up with excitement, and she took his hand and squeezed it. 'Oh, Turi! I want to see them!'

'Of course. Where are you living?'

'We're visiting New York. We have an apartment in Washington.'

'Washington?' Turi's smile faded, and his dark eyes hooded. He searched in his pockets for a cigarette, found one, and turned away from Alessa to light it out of the wind. When he turned back to her his expression was grim. 'We must talk again.'

'Why, of course we will!'

'That's not what I mean. You must do something for me. And not just for me. For thousands, perhaps. Where is your hotel?'

She told him.

'Good, I know it. Two blocks east is an Italian pastry and coffee shop. You can't miss it. It's got a red awning with "Angelo's" lettered in gold. Meet me there at ten o'clock tonight. Don't tell your husband where you are going.'

'This must be terribly important.'

'Life and death, *cara mia*, life and death.'

ONE

'Please tell me you've got hamburgers today,' I said, browsing the grease-spotted menu.

'Yes, ma'am,' the colored waitress, whose name I already knew was 'Jonesy', answered, pulling a pencil from behind her ear and suspending it over her order pad, 'but they won't last long.'

So I hadn't dreamed the sizzle of beef fat on the grill and the odor of frying red meat that struck me when I walked into the diner.

'Thank goodness. I'll have a cheeseburger, medium, French fries, and a glass of milk. And I'm expecting someone to join me.'

'Yes, ma'am,' Jonesy said.

The diner was hot and close with the body heat of hungry people crammed into booths. Steam fogged the plate glass window that fronted Pennsylvania Avenue. Happily, the smell of grilled onions and frying bacon disguised the odor of people who couldn't bathe or wash their clothes as often as they'd like. If you lived in a boarding house with a dozen other people your time in the bathroom was limited.

Alessa di Luca sat down opposite me in the booth, sliding across the seat and tugging off the heavy coat I'd seen her wear every Friday evening for a month. And I thought, for the umpteenth time, that it looked like a man's discarded greatcoat she'd picked up at a thrift shop. One button didn't match the others, and the seat fabric was rubbed shiny from wear.

'Am I late?' she asked.

'Not at all. But I ordered already. I could not wait! They have hamburgers and cheese-burgers!'

Jonesy appeared at Alessa's side.

'If you still have hamburgers, I want one,' Alessa said.

'We do, ma'am,' Jonesy said. 'But they're going fast.'

'Well done, please,' Alessa said.

'Fries with that?'

'No thanks. Coffee if you've got it. With lots of milk.'

I didn't know Alessa well, but I liked her very much. We'd been casual friends since we met at a Friday night knitting circle I attended, where she generously repaired my frequent dropped stitches. We'd had coffee together a couple of times. Last night she'd asked me to have lunch with her today, and I was happy to spend time with someone congenial I

14

didn't work or live with.

Alessa was a war refugee who spoke English fluently with an Italian accent. Despite her thrift shop clothing she had soft hands, perfect skin and lovely manners, so I assumed she was a gentlewoman in 'distressed circumstances', waiting until the end of the war to discover if she could return to Italy, or if her home even existed any more. Thousands upon thousands of refugees from all over the world like her waited in dread, with a spark of hope, for news of their homes and loved ones.

So I didn't know Alessa's story, and I didn't ask. In Washington, DC, in November of 1942, no one had time for such pleasantries. Besides, it was none of my business, and I was accustomed to secrets.

'You got our last hamburger, ma'am,' Jonesy said to Alessa as she set our plates in front of us and poured fresh coffee for Alessa.

The new arrivals in the booth behind us heard her, and a hum of disappointment and frustration rose and fell, as they adjusted to getting grilled cheese sandwiches or hot dogs for lunch.

I tucked into my burger. I was hungry. Dellaphine, the cook and housekeeper at my boarding house, didn't prepare any meals on the weekend except Sunday dinner. I'd eaten a single slice of toast, without jam even, for

15

breakfast. I wasn't complaining, mind you. I felt lucky to live at 'Two Trees', where I got breakfast and dinner during the week, had my own bedroom and shared a bathroom with Phoebe and Ada.

My cheeseburger, topped with a thick slice of fried onion and sweet pickle relish, tasted heavenly, and the salty fries weren't the new mealy frosted kind, but fresh-cut and crisp, with the skin on. I ate half of what was on my plate before I paused.

'This is a popular place,' Alessa said, looking around. Every booth and counter stool was full, and a dozen people waited near the door for a seat.

'There are so many boarding houses in the neighborhood,' I said. 'You can hardly get in for breakfast during the week. And the food's not too greasy.'

'I'm not particular,' she said.

'Who can be?' I said.

'No one. We must remember those who have nothing to eat at all, and be grateful.'

I searched for a topic of conversation. Not easy, when so much of my life was off-limits.

'What part of Italy are you from?' I asked.

'Not Italy, Sicily,' she said. 'Our island hasn't always been part of Italy. We Sicilians are sensitive about our heritage. We even have our own language, although only the country people speak it now. I could tolerate Mussolini, but I left after the Nazis came to

16

build their air bases and the bombings began. I stay with my mother's cousin here. I suppose you would call me a poor relation.'

'I have a dear friend who's a refugee on Malta,' I said. 'The Nazis bomb it every day. Every single day.' I'd gotten two letters from Rachel after she'd escaped to Malta. She insisted she and her children were safe. I chose to believe that for my own sake, since I'd done everything I could for them.

'The Germans bomb Malta from their bases in Sicily, and the British bomb Sicily from their bases on Malta,' Alessa said. 'Yet the islands are less than a hundred kilometers apart. The situation would be absurd if it weren't monstrous. And our little island is so very lovely. Sometimes I daydream that I'm picnicking on a bluff overlooking the Gulf of Palermo, where there are only fishing boats, no warships, drifting at anchor, eating *focaccia*, sipping *limoncello* and listening to the breeze rustling through the leaves of lemon and almond trees.'

'I'm so sorry,' I said.

'With God's help I'll go home some day.'

'What part of Sicily are you from?' I asked.

'Near Palermo,' she said. 'But I cannot say more.'

'I understand,' I said. 'I didn't mean to pry. I'm from Wilmington, North Carolina, myself.'

'The South? Where the cotton plantations

are?'

'Wilmington's on the coast. We make our living from shipbuilding and fishing.'

'You came here to work for the government?'

'Yes, soon after Pearl Harbor.' Washington, DC, once a sleepy southern city, was now a boom town crammed with soldiers and sailors. Washingtonians repeated constantly the wisecrack that DC was an occupied city – occupied by its own troops! Not to mention thousands of government workers, job seekers, drifters, prostitutes, con men, pickpockets and just plain hoodlums. Washington's homicide rate was more than twice New York City's!

'So, busy as you must be with your job, what inspired you to take up knitting?' Alessa asked.

Smile crinkles formed at the corners of her brown eyes, and her mouth turned up in an impish grin. Despite her troubles Alessa still had a sense of humor!

'Because I'm so good at it?' I grinned back. 'You're awfully nice to correct my mistakes every single week!'

'Don't be silly,' she said. 'I'm sure you are very competent ... at something else!' We both laughed out loud.

'Oh, I don't know why I bother,' I said, 'but there's all this talk about the need for socks in Europe. Maybe I should switch to scarves.

18

They're easier.'

'It doesn't matter what your socks look like,' she said, 'as long as they are warm.' Without knowing it Alessa repeated what Joe, the refugee Czech who boarded with me at 'Two Trees', said every time he noticed me struggling with my knitting needles and yarn.

There were people waiting for our table, but I wasn't ready to head home yet. I wondered what the two of us could do for fun this afternoon. I could hardly ask Alessa to go shopping with me; it was obvious she had little money. I wondered if she'd let me treat her to a movie ticket.

Alessa noticed me glancing at the queue of people waiting for a table. 'We should go,' she said. 'But first.'

She leaned far across the table toward me, took my hand, and lowered her voice.

'I know where you work,' she said.

'Pardon me?' I said. Stunned, I felt my heart leap with alarm. Had I slipped up somewhere? Dropped a clue in the midst of some random conversation?

Alessa sat back in her seat and rummaged in her handbag, pulled out a stubby pencil, and printed three letters on a clean napkin. She turned the napkin toward me, and I saw ... *OSS*. The Office of Strategic Services.

'How did you know?' I asked.

'It was easy,' she said. 'I followed you to

your boarding house after knitting circle ended last week. Then Monday morning I got up quite early, stationed myself outside the house, and followed you to work.'

'The building's not marked.'

'I stopped at a diner across the street and asked the waitress who worked in your building. She said it was full of spies! Besides, there's an army camped outside!' That would be the Army squadron that bivouacked on OSS grounds to guard us. Attracted attention to us, too!

The chatter of the customers, Benny Goodman blaring from the jukebox, the clatter of pots and pans, and the shouted orders of the waitresses to the cooks all receded, until it was just Alessa and me, as if we were crowded together in a phone booth on an empty street. I was aware of no emotion except caution. Who was this woman, and what did she want from me? My training kicked in.

'I'm a just file clerk,' I said.

'Dear Louise,' she said, 'you are not an ordinary government girl. You're educated. And older. You have an important boss, no?'

Why pretend? 'Yes,' I said.

'I have something you must give to him.' She pulled a thin leaflet, folded in half, out of her bag and handed it to me. 'Here is the knitting pattern I promised you,' she said, so loudly that I guessed she wanted our neighbors in the next booth to hear. Of course I reached for the leaflet, and she pressed it into my hand, gripping it for a second before she turned it loose.

Alessa got to her feet and struggled into her heavy coat. 'So I'll see you Friday night, for the knitting?' she said.

'I'll be there,' I said.

She strolled calmly out of the diner, leaving me astonished by her audacity.

By now the waiting diners huddled inside the door were glaring nastily at me, so I hastened to leave my booth, tucking the leaflet carefully into my handbag.

When I tossed a dime on the table for Jonesy's tip I noticed that Alessa had left half of her burger uneaten.

TWO

As I turned into the tiny front yard of my boarding house, I reflexively checked the front window to see if both the stars taped on it were still blue. My landlady, Phoebe Holcombe, had two sons in the Navy in the Pacific fighting the Japs. We all dreaded coming home one day to find a gold star in her window.

Inside I hung up my coat and stowed my galoshes under the coat tree. Instead of dropping my handbag on the hall chair I kept it over my arm, instinctively protecting Alessa's note. I could hear my fellow boarders talking in the lounge with the radio playing quietly in the background, but I was too unnerved to make small talk with them. I slipped down the hall toward the kitchen, Dellaphine's domain, where I found her ironing one of Phoebe's housecoats.

'Hello, Mrs Pearlie,' Dellaphine said. 'Did you have a nice lunch?'

'Yes, I did,' I answered. 'The diner had hamburgers.' My voice cracked a bit, and Dellaphine looked at me curiously.

'You all right?' she asked.

'I don't feel well,' I said. An understatement, considering a foreign refugee I barely knew had figured out I worked for OSS and given me a message to take to my superiors. And there was not a damn thing I could do about it until I went to work on Monday morning.

'You look like you seen a ghost.'

'Dellaphine, could I have a shot of bourbon? Please?'

'Sure. You do look peaked.' Dellaphine winked at me, then pulled a key ring out of her apron pocket and unlocked the pantry cabinet that stored an impressive stash of the late Mr Holcombe's favorite bourbons and Phoebe's sherry. Phoebe wouldn't permit her boarders to bring their own liquor into the house, but she allowed Dellaphine to dole out what alcohol she locked in the pantry.

Dellaphine handed me an orange juice glass with about a jigger of Old Grand-Dad in it and then relocked the cabinet. She went back to ironing without asking me any more questions.

I drained it in two swallows.

'Better?' Dellaphine asked.

'Definitely,' I said. I went over to the kitchen sink and washed the glass, leaving it on the drainboard to dry.

'I'm going to my room to lie down,' I said.

'You get some rest. You work too hard.'

Once in my room I sank on to my bed and rummaged through my handbag for the leaflet Alessa had given me. It was a knitting pattern, all right, but tucked inside was a small envelope. It wasn't sealed, so I removed and unfolded a page torn from a pad of school-ruled paper. Tiny words in Italian, written in blue ink with one of those new ballpoint pens, crowded the page. No letterhead, no salutation, no signature, just sentences crammed on to the page from top to bottom and edge-to-edge. A few more sentences, also in Italian, written in pencil in a different hand, squeezed into the narrow margin at the bottom of the page. I couldn't understand a word of it.

My mind raced with curiosity. If I had any brains I'd be scared, I told myself. This Alessa woman knew who I was and where I lived, and that I worked for America's spy agency.

'Louise?' Ada's voice followed her tap on my door. 'Dearie, are you all right?'

Quickly, I refolded the paper, stuffed it into its envelope, and slid it back into my pocketbook.

'Sure,' I answered, 'come on in.'

Ada was on her way to work at the Willard Hotel where she played in the house band. She wore expertly applied make-up and a sea green silk dress. A snood glittering with rhinestones enclosed her shoulder length dyed platinum blonde hair. She carried an evening bag and her clarinet case.

'Dellaphine said you didn't feel well,' Ada said.

'I'm OK. A little under the weather.'

'I was hoping you might come over to the hotel later on,' she said. 'I get a few hours off between the tea dance and our evening gig. We could have a couple of Martinis and dinner.'

'Ada, you know how I feel about that.'

'You're so old-fashioned!'

'Look, when women sit around in a bar without a date you know what men think.'

'So?'

'I don't like being propositioned by drunken soldiers and traveling salesmen.'

'You'd rather scramble an egg and read some mystery book?'

'Yes, I would.' Especially if Joe was around.

'OK,' she said. 'It's your life.'

Yes, it is, I thought to myself as I listened to Ada click down the stairs in her high heels. And I intended to live it my way. I liked Ada, but I didn't want to be drawn into her life of cocktails and never-ending stream of boyfriends. Sometimes I wondered if she wanted me around so she could keep an eye on me for fear I'd blurt out her secret. In a moment of despair she'd confided in me that before the war she'd married a German commercial airline pilot who was now a Nazi officer in the Luftwaffe. She was terrified of being discovered and imprisoned in an internment camp. She didn't dare even file for divorce.

Hers wasn't the only secret I kept. When we were alone, which was rare, I teased Joe that he was 'undercover'. The others thought he was a language teacher – he made a big show of writing lectures and grading papers. By accident I'd found out that he worked for a humanitarian agency, raising money, scrounging for ship berths, and supplying safe houses, all to help European Jews escape the Nazis. He'd constructed an identity as a language teacher to protect his family still in Czechoslovakia. Prager wasn't his real name. It was Czech for 'Prague'.

And, of course, I'd locked my memory tight shut on the foolish risks I'd taken to help Rachel Bloch and her children escape from Vichy France hours before the Gestapo entered Marseilles. If anyone at OSS knew what I'd done I'd have at least lost my job and possibly wound up in the federal women's prison in West Virginia. Which I might actually prefer to going home and back to gutting bluefish and frying hush puppies at my parents' fish camp on the Cape Fear River.

Luckily, I'd always known how to keep my mouth shut.

THREE

Enzo kept the deepest secret of Alessa's life: one that if revealed would ruin her and perhaps cost her brother his life. And all for only three dollars a week!

Alessa had met Enzo when she'd come upon him on a cigarette break outside the hotel near the servants' entrance. His hands were filthy, and he wore a hotel apron stiff with silver tarnish. Normally, she wouldn't have spoken to him, but she was desperate for a cigarette herself. When she asked him for a light in Italian, he answered her in Sicilian. After he lit her cigarette they talked. He was an illiterate tradesman's son from a tiny village near her home in Ficuzza. He'd immigrated to the United States almost ten years ago. With thousands of others he'd fled Sicily in the thirties, when Mussolini consolidated his power on the island. His uncle had found him a job in the hotel. Alessa realized immediately that Enzo was a man of honor, who valued the Tradition above all else, and because of that he would protect her secrets without hesitation. As long as he got his three dollars. So she told him what

27

she needed from him.

Enzo toiled in the vast sub-basement of the massive hotel in the silver room, where he polished hundreds of pieces of silverware and silver plate every day. He procured a key to the servants' entrance and a secluded employee's locker for her use.

After lunch with Louise Alessa walked back to the hotel, ducked into the servants' entrance and went to her secret locker. She changed out of her thrift shop disguise and into a tweed suit and pumps, slipped on her rings and bracelets, pulled on leather gloves, adjusted her hat, and applied a bit of make-up. She hung her old clothes neatly in the locker and locked it.

Alessa waited outside the door to the street until no one was in sight, then slipped out of the servants' entrance and on to the sidewalk. Quickly, she went around the corner on to De Sales Street and into the residents' private entrance. The doorman opened the door for her, and she approached the concierge's desk.

'Good afternoon, ma'am,' he said, bowing his head slightly.

'And to you, Hays,' she said. 'Can you tell me if my husband is in?'

'Yes, I believe he is. But your mother-in-law has gone to the lounge for tea with friends, I believe.' Alessa suspected sherry was more likely.

Thank God, Alessa thought. Perhaps Orazio would be out on one of his many errands too. It was rare these days for Alessa to have time alone with her darling husband Sebastian.

FOUR

A clang sounded from the cold water pipe that ran down a corner of my bedroom from the sink in Joe and Henry's attic room all the way to the cellar. Since Phoebe would have evicted us if she ever found either me in the attic or Joe on our floor, he and I communicated through the water pipe. One clang meant: 'Can you meet me downstairs?' Two meant: 'No.' Three meant: 'Good night, darling.' The darling part was my own interpretation, you understand.

Of course, we used our code only if Henry wasn't upstairs with Joe in the bedroom they shared. He would have informed on us for sure. I tapped the pipe twice. I had too much on my mind to deal with Joe and my confused feelings for him tonight.

I waited in my room until I heard Joe and Henry leave the house to find dinner. That left the house nearly empty. Phoebe and I ate scrambled eggs alone in the dining room while Dellaphine and her daughter, Madeleine, fixed themselves ham sandwiches and ate in the kitchen.

On Saturday nights I had the lounge to myself to enjoy the Grand Ole Opry. I liked Glen Miller and Tommy Dorsey and swing and crooning and all, but I was a country girl and I missed the Carter family, Patsy Cline, and Roy Acuff. While lying prone on Phoebe's threadbare davenport, I closed my eyes and listened to Hank Williams sing 'Lovesick Blues'. As I relaxed my head cleared and I was able to think calmly about my lunch with Alessa.

Was it so awful that Alessa had found out I worked at OSS? We government girls were trained to answer 'I'm a file clerk in a government office' to any inquiries, but how hard could it be to find out what my office did? And like she said, most everyone knew that my branch of OSS occupied the huge old apartment building on 'E' street, and dozens of us walked openly through its doors every day. And that letter she gave me probably contained nothing of critical interest to anyone. Refugees mobbed the Washington bureaucracy daily, desperately trying to find out the fates of their families, their homes, and their friends. Alessa might have a scrap of information she wanted to trade for some favor. Don Murray, who headed my branch's Europe/Africa desk, would accept Alessa's missive from me and toss it in the in-box of one of his researchers who could read Italian. Nothing would come of it. When I next saw Alessa I could tell her I'd done as she asked, and that would be the end of it.

I was ashamed of the thrill I'd felt when Alessa pressed her note into my hand. So silly of me! What did I think I was, a spy?

Joe was waiting for me at the foot of the stairs when I came down Sunday morning. We were alone in the hall, so he slipped an arm around my waist and pulled me to him. Not for a kiss, but to show me the morning newspaper.

'Look,' he said. 'It's started.'

Every headline on the front page of *The Washington Post* trumpeted the beginning of Operation Torch. Finally, Britain and the United States, a year after the United States declared war on Germany, attacked the Nazis. Three Allied joint task forces landed at Casablanca, Oran, and Algeria. Their goal was to invade French North Africa, recruit the Vichy French forces to the Allied cause, and pin Rommel between the invading force and the British Eighth Army in Egypt, driving the Nazis out of North Africa. From there the Allies could stage an invasion of southern Europe.

Through our work Joe and I were prepared for this. But still it was thrilling. As if the war to free Europe had finally begun.

Joe led me into the empty dining room and

pulled me into his arms. I let myself relax into his body, and we held each other tight as long as we dared. The sound of Henry whooping in the hall drove us apart.

Henry charged into the dining room, pumping his arms in the air. 'Finally! Finally!' he said. 'It's about damn time! If the Republicans were in charge, this would have happened months ago!'

Joe and I didn't bother arguing with him. Instead we went into the kitchen for our allotted cup of coffee.

Since Dellaphine didn't fix breakfast on Sunday mornings the first person up made coffee and one of us who could cook threw something together for everyone to eat. Phoebe or I often fixed biscuits. Sometimes Henry prepared pancakes. We made do with honey instead of jam or syrup.

In the kitchen I found Phoebe sobbing while she sifted flour into a mixing bowl. Ada had a hand on her arm, trying to calm her. Phoebe's sons were in the Pacific, but talk of war anywhere reminded her of the danger they were in.

'Let me do that,' I said, taking the sifter from her and pulling the mixing bowl toward me. I finished sifting the flour and added lard, cutting the two ingredients together with a pastry mixer until they formed little crumbles. Ada measured the baking powder and salt, and then the milk and water for me.

I mixed the batter with a wooden spoon and then kneaded it in the bowl. Phoebe dried her eyes on a tea towel while she watched us. Joe assumed the role of comforter, whispering quietly to her with an arm around her shoulder. She nodded, still with an occasional tear sliding down a cheek.

Despite helping me with the biscuits Ada hadn't said a word yet this morning and was as white as the flour she measured for me. I knew what she was thinking. She desperately wanted her husband to die. She had no idea where he was stationed, but I knew she prayed he would perish on some torrid airfield in Africa soon. If he died, she wouldn't ever need to file for divorce, and she'd be spared the embarrassment and humiliation of revealing her marriage to a Nazi.

The commotion in the kitchen brought Dellaphine and Madeleine upstairs. Dellaphine was dressed for church, wearing her Sunday suit, a black hat decorated with a blackbird wing, sensible shoes, and an enormous handbag. Madeleine wore jeans with the cuffs turned up, a baggy pink sweater, bobby socks, and sneakers. She was one of the first colored girls to find a government job, typing Social Security cards, and she enjoyed the benefits of a regular paycheck, just as I did.

'Why, Miss Phoebe,' Dellaphine said, patting Phoebe's hand. 'What's wrong? Are the

34

boys all right?'

'Milt and Tom are fine,' I said. 'But we've invaded French North Africa.'

'That's no reason for you to be crying, Miss Phoebe,' Dellaphine said. 'That's way on the other side of the world from where the boys are.'

Phoebe dried her eyes again on the same kitchen towel, visibly damp from her tears. 'Oh, I know,' she said. 'But other people's sons are going to die. It's all so terribly sad.'

'Why are we invading Africa, anyway?' Dellaphine said.

'From there it's not far to Italy, Mama,' Madeleine said. 'If you read the newspapers you'd know that.'

'I don't need to read no newspapers,' Dellaphine said. 'I trust God and President Roosevelt to win this war for us.'

Madeleine glanced heavenward, and her mother saw it. She rested a hand on her hip. 'Missy,' she said, 'I can't make you go to church no more, but don't you roll those eyes at me!'

'I'm sorry, Momma,' Madeleine said, deciding for once to avoid an argument.

'Are you fixin' enough biscuits for Sunday dinner, too?' Dellaphine asked me.

'Yes, General Dellaphine, I am,' I answered. I dumped the dough out on the floured wooden pastry board, rolled it out and started cutting it into rounds with the lid of a

Mason jar.

'Do we have any real jam left, Dellaphine?' Phoebe asked.

'Yes, ma'am,' she said, rooting around in the Hoosier cabinet. 'Here, it's peach. Half a jar.'

'I think we will have some this morning.'

Madeleine found a baking pan for me in the pantry, but not without a crash or two.

'Every one of you is a mess,' Dellaphine said. 'It's a good thing you got me to pray for you!'

Shaking her head, Dellaphine went on out the back door and marched off to the Gethsemane Baptist Church. Church for her lasted a good two and a half hours, what with Sunday school, hymns, the sermon, and a social afterwards.

'I should get dressed for church, too,' Phoebe said. Phoebe was an Episcopalian. Her church didn't start for another hour and would be finished promptly in fifty minutes.

'By the time you come back downstairs these will be ready,' I said, shoving the tray of biscuits in the oven.

'I don't think I could eat,' Phoebe said. 'I'll take a cup of coffee upstairs with me.'

When the biscuits came out of the oven, golden and hot, we smeared them with thin layers of butter and jam. Ada, Joe and I took ours into the lounge to eat while reading every page of *The Washington Post*. Henry

36

subscribed to the *Washington Herald*, the conservative newspaper, so he had it all to himself. The rest of us, including Phoebe, were New Dealers. Madeleine carried her biscuits and coffee downstairs to her room, where she'd read the *Baltimore Afro-American*, the biggest colored newspaper on the east coast.

When Phoebe got home from church she managed to eat half a biscuit, but she avoided the front pages of the *Post*, concentrating instead on the funny pages and the women's section.

As soon as Dellaphine got home she changed into a house dress and tied on her apron to fix Sunday dinner. Phoebe insisted that as long as she was alive there'd be Sunday dinner at her house. We boarders were so grateful to be living in luxury compared to most of the jam-packed boarding houses in the city that we were happy to pitch in and help with the chores. Ada set the table, and I helped Dellaphine cook. Joe dried the dishes, a sight that stunned us all when he first did it. I'd never seen a man near a kitchen sink before in my life. Women's work was beneath Henry, but he did take care of Phoebe's car and the yard.

Ada and I often wondered why Phoebe took in boarders, aside from the patriotism of it. We didn't think it was for the money. Mr Holcombe lost plenty during the

Depression and subsequently died in an accident, which Dellaphine hinted was suicide. But Phoebe must have some money of her own, because she'd kept the house and sent her sons to college. We'd concluded that we boarders somehow took the place of Phoebe's sons, that we filled up the house and allowed a semblance of normalcy for both Dellaphine and Phoebe. Running a boarding house kept them both busy.

Whatever the reason, we were happy to sit down in the middle of Sunday afternoon and eat fried chicken and mashed potatoes with cream sauce, scalloped cabbage, and leftover biscuits. Dessert was cherry jello embedded with canned pineapple. When I'd first arrived here we would have had cake or pie, but those days were long gone.

What was left of Sunday afternoon passed quietly. No matter what I did, knitting or reading, I couldn't stop thinking about Alessa and the letter she'd given to me. I had mixed feelings about the incident. On the one hand I wanted to get to work tomorrow early, pass the letter on to Don, and forget about it. When I next saw Alessa I could tell her I'd done what she'd asked and go back to knitting socks badly. Then again I was desperately curious. I wanted to know the contents of that letter and why Alessa wanted to contact OSS.

As six o'clock approached we drifted into

the lounge to listen to the news. We settled in our accustomed seats on Phoebe's outdated furniture with its worn upholstery. Henry turned on the radio.

'I think we could all use a sherry, don't you?' Phoebe asked, coming into the room with her favorite crystal sherry glasses, filled to the brim, on a silver tray. Yes, we could. We sipped as we listened, first to Edward R. Murrow and then the news program on WINX. Our elation over 'Torch' turned to worry as we listened to the enormous scope of the invasion. A massive armada, thousands of men, countless tanks and airplanes, streamed across the Atlantic and into North Africa, and for what? To gain a foothold on a piece of land from where we might, might, be able to invade southern Europe?

I glanced at Joe. His dark beard hid much of his face, making him look older than he was, but as he bent over his pipe to light it, I could swear I saw tears glisten in his eyes.

'I hope Roosevelt has the guts to give Patton his head! This Eisenhower guy is too damn cautious,' Henry said. 'We could be in Berlin by spring!'

'Not likely,' Joe said, drawing on his pipe until the bowl glowed. 'First we have to beat Rommel. There's no guarantee we will. The man is brilliant. Then we must invade Europe and fight our way to Berlin. And we can't get there directly from Italy because of the Alps and Switzerland. Hitler will defend every inch of territory. It will be–' and he sought for the appropriate words in English – 'bloody and vicious. Europe will be rubble by the time it's over.'

I knew Joe was wondering how many refugees his organization could get out of Europe before the next bloodbath began.

'Don't forget the Japs,' Ada said. 'We have to beat them too.'

'Hell, of course we will!' Henry said. 'America's never lost a war.'

I hoped to God he was right. It was too horrific to contemplate, the Japanese in control of the Pacific and Hitler ruling Europe. What kind of world would that be for our children to live in?

And then I thought of Rachel. She, baby Louisa, and little Claude had found refuge in the grotto abbey of the Little Sisters of the Poor in Hamrun, Malta. Once the allies conquered North Africa, the daily bombings of Malta would stop. Wouldn't they?

None of us slept well that night. I know because when I went downstairs for a glass of water I found Phoebe sipping sherry in the kitchen and saw Joe out on the chilly porch, smoking his pipe, in a worn dressing gown with a blanket thrown over his shoulders.

40

FIVE

I pushed the heavy file cart into Don's office and closed the door behind me.

'Good morning, Mrs Pearlie,' Don said, raising his eyes from the stack of papers on his desk. 'You're early. I'm done with those,' he said, nodding at the table piled with files that stood under his office window.

Don Murray had aged since taking over the Europe/Africa desk. Strands of gray streaked his hair. His eyes were often bloodshot. He carried home a full briefcase at night and was the first person in the office every morning.

I unloaded my trolley and stacked files on to his desk in a pile so high it teetered, then emptied his OUT box of an equally towering mountain of paper. When I returned to my office I'd sort through the mountain and either file all that paper or redirect it to other crowded desks.

'Mr Murray,' I said, wiping my hands on the damp cloth I kept on the trolley, 'I need to speak to you.'

'What is it, Louise?' he said, slipping into

41

using my first name. We'd dated once before his promotion. 'I'm awfully busy. And I don't see how I can get you another clerk. State and the War Department are sucking up all the manpower in the District.'

'I've been contacted by a floater,' I said. 'Floater' was spy lingo for a civilian who becomes part of an intelligence operation.

'What?' he said, taking off his glasses and leaning back in his chair. 'Who? How did he know you work here?'

'She.'

I sat down at his desk and told him the entire story. After he heard me out he scanned the page of Italian I'd given him.

'Well,' he said, 'interesting. But I doubt this will amount to much.'

I'd learned from the time I was a little girl that I couldn't say out loud much of what crossed my mind, if I wanted to keep a job or a man or my good name. But I could think whatever I liked, and did. Of course Don assumed Alessa's information was insignificant. I was a file clerk. Alessa was a penniless female refugee. We'd met at a knitting circle. This was all Don's male mind needed, to conclude that Alessa's letter would turn out to be insignificant.

'I'll have this translated,' he said. 'In the meantime, when do you expect to see this woman again?'

'Friday evening. At our knitting circle.'

'I'll brief you on how to handle the contact before then.'

'Yes, sir.' I'm sure you will.

'Thank you, Mrs Pearlie,' Don said, dismissing me, already settling his glasses on his nose and opening another file.

I was the Chief File Clerk of the Europe/Africa Section of the Research and Analysis Branch of the Office of Strategic Services. Which was an impressive way of saying that I was responsible for all the paper the section generated. And did we ever generate paper, tons of it when multiplied by dozens of offices like mine scattered throughout the OSS compound. Nine hundred people worked in the old apartment house that held R&A. Most of our scholars/spies were renowned academics – economists, historians, anthropologists, linguists, and scientists – recruited from American universities, mostly Harvard and Yale. Some were foreign experts who'd fled their countries ahead of the Nazis. Our researchers studied everything from covert intelligence gathered by agents all over the world, to muddy underground newsletters picked up on the streets of occupied foreign cities, to National Geographic maps, to decades-old tourist guides, to interviews with expatriates. Many camped at the Library of Congress, scouring it for usable information. The rest of us, the file clerks, all women, typed, filed, sorted, and distributed the material generated by this army of eggheads.

The operational branches of OSS, the glamour boys and girls, called us the 'chair borne brigade', but without the information we analyzed, our spies in the field, and the armies that followed them, would have been deaf, dumb, and blind. It was because of our work that they landed on foreign soil with current maps, phrase books, enemy positions, and resistance contacts.

Which is why I'd expected the news about Torch we'd read in the newspapers yesterday. For months we'd been typing and filing reports on everything from how to greet a Mohammedan mullah to the track gauges of Tunisian railways. During our busiest weeks we soaked our overworked hands in hot water and Epsom salts every night. And we couldn't nearly do it all. At night the researchers sneaked in wives and girlfriends to type and collate. We'd find neat stacks of reports outside our door every morning.

I shoved open my office door with my hip and pushed the heavy file cart inside, where Ruth, my filing whizz, was alphabetizing an armful of brown file jackets.

'I need that cart,' she said to me, before even saying hello.

'It's all yours. And Mr Murray is done with these folders,' I said. 'They need to be returned to the files.'

'And these,' she said, nodding to another stack of files. 'I think they'll all fit.'

We loaded up the file cart, and she was out the door.

Ruth may have once been a spoiled Mount Holyoke deb with a wardrobe of silk dresses and two strands of pearls, but now she wore trousers and twisted her hair up off her face. She could file faster and more accurately than any of us. I expect she dreamed about the alphabet at night.

Now, Betty, a hare-brained blonde in search of a husband in uniform – any uniform, any rank – was my crackerjack typist. She could read everyone's handwriting, even the foreigners', and type accurately through ten sheets of carbon paper with barely a mistake. An important skill, because each error needed to be erased from all the copies under all those sheets of carbon paper. Although life had become easier when William Langer, our new branch director, had decreed that a few strikeouts in long single-spaced documents were permissible.

When Brenda Bonner arrived, I'd thought she must have lied about her age to personnel. She looked like Dorothy in *The Wizard of Oz* with her long brown pigtails and checked jumper. But she'd taken her first paycheck straight to Penney's and bought trousers and dark sweaters, all the better to hide the newspaper ink that smudged her hands and arms black. She bandaged her right hand to keep blisters from forming as she worked her scissors all day, clipping articles from the stack of newspapers, magazines, and journals that surrounded her desk. For filing, of course.

I reserved most of the indexing for myself. Indexing all those files was critical. Once files were stashed away in the file cabinets that crammed the building, even occupying space in bathrooms, hallways, and cloakrooms, we needed to be able to find them again.

Every file had its own three inch by five inch index card which described the file's location and its subject. Then there were the cross references. Say I was indexing a new file on Ada's Luftwaffe husband. His name, Rein Hermann, would be the main title of the file. But I'd also need to add to his index card the subject titles 'Luftwaffe', 'Nazis who'd lived in the United States', the name of the civilian airline he'd flown with, and so forth. Then the index card would need to be filed properly. And finally Ruth could stow the main file in a file cabinet.

If Ada's husband's name came up again we could find his file. Immediately. A misfiled document might as well not exist.

My girls made the base clerical pay of fourteen hundred and forty dollars a year. I made a little over sixteen hundred dollars. Twice what my husband made as a Western Union telegrapher before he died; more than I ever dreamed possible. My parents wouldn't believe me if I told them. After paying my room and board at Phoebe's, my taxes, and buying a war bond, I had over a hundred dollars a month in my pocket. No matter what I had to do, I would never go back to Wilmington to live, war or no war. I intended to have a career and be independent the rest of my life, whether I remarried or not. I didn't say so out loud, but I thought about it plenty.

Betty threw up her hands. 'Thank God, it's done!' She ripped the paper out of her typewriter and separated the carbons from the copies. The carbons went into the trash to be burned at the end of the day. She added the finished pages to the eight collated piles of the rest of the document and stapled each of them together with a flourish.

She lit a cigarette and inspected her fingers. 'My nails are a mess. I need a manicure in the worst way.'

Ellen stopped scissoring to shake a cramp out of her hand. 'What happens now, Mrs Pearlie?' she asked. 'I mean, now that we've invaded North Africa? To us, I mean.'

'OSS will open an outpost in North Africa and handle OSS business in the region from there,' I said.

'Then what will we do?'

'Begin to prepare for the next stage of the war,' I said.

'What do you think that will be?' Betty said.

Sicily, Sardinia, Italy. 'I don't know,' I said. 'We'll find out soon enough.'

Brenda massaged her hand. 'Go take your break,' I said to her. 'And Betty, when you're done with your cigarette, take those reports to the mail room.'

I grabbed a stack of alphabetized cards and rolled our library ladder over to the first bank of index file drawers. They were stacked from floor to ceiling, and the ceilings were twelve feet high, lining every wall of our office, a gutted two-bedroom apartment. In the main room we could barely move between our desks, the tables stacked with documents, and the massive Yale walk-in floor safe, which held our Top Secret documents.

Our short hall once contained four apartments. A former studio accommodated our security detail: two soldiers who stood at the entrances outside, and a sergeant who checked our visitors in and out. This seemed excessive to me, since an Army squadron was camped outside our building and patrolled the OSS grounds night and day.

Another small apartment had become Don's office. At the end of the hall were the offices of four scholars. Dora Bertrand, an anthropologist, was the only woman I knew with a PhD. I admired her greatly, even though she was in a scandalous Wellesley marriage with another woman. Roger Austine was a French language professor from Tulane whose uncle was the archbishop of Toulouse. He was the talk of our office because he was engaged to a sophisticated mulatto woman from the French Caribbean. Guy Danielson was a conservative, almost a monarchist, and a historian from Princeton. He and Roger loathed each other. I didn't know Jack Singer well. He was an economist who'd taken Don's place when he was promoted.

This pattern, a cluster of scholars supported by clerical staff, repeated itself dozens of times throughout the building.

As I clambered up and down my ladder, I admitted to myself that I felt disappointed. Let down, even. I'd magnified what my contact with Alessa might mean, and Don's diffidence deflated me. My adventure helping Rachel leave Vichy was terrifying, even dangerous, and I was so relieved that it was over. But I missed the excitement of it, the relief from the drudgery of the files.

For a woman I had a good education and an important job. I had a junior college degree. I had Top Secret Clearance. I made a salary that would have been a fantasy a year ago. I no longer relied on my parents for a roof over my head. I no longer felt the pressure to remarry after Bill had died in order to get out of my parents' house. But I wanted more. I wanted to use all my brains, not just the part that knew the alphabet!

Dora Bertrand, who would return to her faculty position at Smith College after the war, had promised to help me finish college. I wouldn't let her forget!

The next morning Don met me at the door to my office.

'Mrs Pearlie,' he said, 'we're having a quick meeting in my office. Could you come take notes, please?'

'Of course,' I said. 'Let me get my note-book.'

I threw my coat down on my desk, picked up a steno pad and pencil, and told the girls where I'd be.

As I followed Don down the hall to his office, I noticed he was wearing the same clothes he'd worn yesterday. He must have slept on the cot in his office. I wondered what was up.

Dora, Jack, Roger, and Guy were not waiting for us in Don's office. Two strange men were there instead. Well, they weren't strangers, I'd seen them in the OSS cafeteria, but I didn't know who they were.

Both men stood up and extended their

hands. The younger one shook my hand first.

'Mrs Pearlie,' he said, 'I'm Max Corso, Secret Intelligence Branch, Italian section.'

'And I'm Platon Melinsky,' the second man said. 'Also Secret Intelligence.'

'Please take a seat, Mrs Pearlie,' Don said.

'Cigarette?' Corso asked me.

'No, thank you, I don't smoke.'

Corso lit his and inhaled deeply while I wondered what brought the head of the SI Italian desk to Don's office.

'Mrs Pearlie, have you heard of Operation Underworld?' Corso asked.

Of course I'd heard of Operation Underworld. I was well briefed on most OSS activities through my access to our section's files and ladies' restroom gossip. The men in the office must think the clerical staff was deaf, dumb, and blind.

'Operation Underworld,' I said, choosing my words carefully. I didn't want to reveal how well informed I was. 'The Office of Naval Intelligence recruited the Mafia to protect the Port of New York City.'

'Through the unions they control,' Corso said. 'The Teamsters, the longshoremen, restaurant workers, even the stallholders at the Fulton Fish Market. Most of these union members are Italian Americans. They detest Mussolini and the Nazis. They're watching the docks and Allied ships, eavesdropping on foreign nationals, spying on incoming vessels, even monitoring our fishing fleet. The dockyards are full of spies working for the Nazis, and only the Mafia has the resources to blanket the Port.'

'The spies aren't Americans!' I said.

'There are a few Italian Americans who support Mussolini,' Corso said, 'but not many, and we know who most of them are. Our real problems are the sleepers – operatives the Nazis and Mussolini planted secretly on the dockyards before the war started. We don't know how many they are, but we do know they are funneling information to the Nazis.'

'The Office of Naval Intelligence needed the unions and the Mafia to have any hope of securing the docks,' Don said. 'We're talking about hundreds of square miles of piers, warehouses, and depots. Not to mention the US Naval Shipyard. So the ONI contacted "Lucky" Luciano. Cardinal Spellman was their go-between.'

'I thought Luciano was in Dannemora prison?'

'He is,' Corso said. 'But his *capibastone*, his underbosses, Frank Costello and "Socks" Lanza, aren't. Neither is his *consigliere*, Meyer Lansky. No one in the world hates Nazis more than Lansky.'

'Does this have something to do with Alessa's letter?'

'Yes,' Don said, 'but let us begin at the beginning, and we'll get to the letter later. Platon?'

'What do you know about the New York City dock system?' Melinsky asked me.

I'd been trying not to stare at Melinsky, but now I had an excuse to face him. The man was famous, if not infamous, at OSS. His aristocratic, self-assured bearing corresponded with everything I'd heard about him. He was tall, slim, and as athletic as a man must be who trained as a paratrooper in his fifties. I'd heard rumors that his Army uniforms were tailor-made.

'What everyone else knows, I guess,' I said.

'The New York City docks are the most vulnerable part of the eastern seaboard. The Port handles half of all US foreign trade. Two hundred cargo docks, warehouses, and piers in Manhattan, Queens, New Jersey, and Brooklyn cover eighty miles. Our troop ships depart from there. Most of the supplies we send to our Allies in Europe are sent from the Port of New York City.'

'The port is vulnerable to espionage and sabotage. The burning of the *Normandy* and Pier Eighty-Three proves that,' Corso said.

'But those were accidents,' I said. 'Weren't they?'

The three men exchanged glances that told me maybe they weren't.

'Doesn't matter,' Don interjected. 'They

happened. The *Normandy* was being converted to a troop carrier. Fifty-six million dollars it cost the government. Gone.'

'Then there are the convoys,' Corso said. 'Without them Britain would starve. And now more will leave the port to support the Torch campaign in North Africa. We know the Germans have advance information about routes and cargoes. This year alone German U-boats have sunk almost one thousand two hundred ships. All the U-boats need to do is line up about fifteen miles apart across a convoy's planned route and start picking off ships after night falls.'

'God or luck is with us in North Africa,' Don said. 'There's an American standard gauge railway that runs from Casablanca to Algiers to Tunis. We can load up railroad cars and send them directly to the front. But only if the supplies and troops can get to Casablanca.'

'The fast convoys have done their job, delivering the initial force to the front. Now the slow convoys must supply them. They can only steam as fast as the slowest ship – under seven knots,' Melinsky said. 'If the U-boats know their routes, those ships are sitting ducks.'

'When do the first slow convoys leave?' Corso asked.

'The week after Thanksgiving,' Don said. His hand shook as he stubbed out his cigarette. He immediately lit another. 'We have to identify and neutralize Axis spies in New York. As many as possible, no matter the cost.'

The three men had succeeded in scaring me badly, but why were they telling me all this? I was just a file clerk, letter or no letter.

'Max?' Don asked. 'You'd better brief her.'

'This is for our ears only,' Max said. 'No notes, please. I'm glad you already have Top Secret Clearance, Mrs Pearlie. That will make this operation possible.'

I was burning with curiosity but managed to compose myself.

'Your friend's asset,' he said, sliding Alessa's letter out of a file on the desk, 'has proved his *bona fides* without doubt.'

'So you must've determined that the information in the letter is genuine,' I said.

'It is,' Corso said. 'But it's chicken feed. The asset is not ready to pass on the critical material – what we call "the take" – he says he possesses yet. He's testing us. He's concerned about the safety of his family and of Alessa. She's a floater, a civilian he recruited to help him, not a professional.'

Melinsky pulled out a packet of Sobranies and lit one. He drew smoke deep into his lungs and exhaled. 'Mrs Pearlie,' he said, 'Alessa di Luca's asset tells us he knows the identity of a dangerous sleeper, a powerful Mafia hoodlum who is feeding intelligence to the Nazis. If it's true it's a catastrophe. He must be stopped. We must find out who he is. And Alessa will deal with no one but you. She makes that clear in the note she added to her asset's letter. So we can't forward this on to the ONI. Not yet, anyway.'

'For a time, at least, you'll need to be the cut-out between Alessa and OSS,' Don said.

My head swam at the thought, and I felt blood rush to my face. I gripped the arms of the chair to steady myself. I was frightened, yes, but I was excited too. I was to be the intermediary between Alessa and OSS. My life wasn't boring any more!

Don and Corso stood up to leave.

'Melinsky here is your case officer. He'll brief you further,' Don said as the two men left his office.

And my case officer was Prince of Imperial Russia Platon Melinsky!

Melinsky's first wife was the last czar's sister, Catherine, and his second was an Astor. He'd fought in the First World War and the Russian Civil War. He immigrated to the United States to join the US Army and fight Hitler. Now he was a lieutenant colonel assigned to OSS. A prince, no less. My handler in my first foray into intelligence.

And then it hit me. I was a real spy. A temporary one, for sure, assigned to Alessa because she wouldn't work with anyone else, but a spy nonetheless. Planted in a knitting circle, of all things. I was floored.

'What about my job?' I asked. 'I mean, my regular job?'

'You'll keep it. Despite the value of Alessa's intelligence you should only have to meet with her a few times before she hands the sleeper's name over to you. I'll brief you on your cover for any absences from work or home and what you are to share with your staff, friends, everyone – and I mean *everyone*, even here at OSS. Forever.'

'I understand.'

Melinsky opened a fresh pack of Sobranies. He lit it with a heavy silver lighter engraved with an insignia that looked like a trident. He saw me looking at it. 'The Rurik coat of arms,' he said to me. 'I'm not a Romanov. The Rurik dynasty failed centuries ago.' The man had a dynasty, for Pete's sake!

'Listen carefully,' Melinsky began. 'This is your cover for your absences from work. An elderly spinster recently died in Bethesda. Her lifetime hobby was collecting European postcards. She received them from friends, bought them, and traded them. Her nephew discovered box after box as he was cleaning out her apartment. He's offered them to the Library of Congress, who has suggested to us that someone from the Research and Analysis sort through these postcards for useful information.'

'Like the locations of railroad stations and bridges.'

'Possible targets, exactly. Don Murray has volunteered you for the job. You'll be gone for a couple of days. And, of course, you'll offer no explanation at all to your friends and family. You'll just say that your job requires you to be out of town for a few days. And maybe occasionally after that.'

'I don't understand. Where am I going?'

'Tell me, Mrs Pearlie, what kind of training do you have?'

'Training? I have a secretarial degree from junior college.'

Melinsky smiled. 'Not that kind of training,' he said. 'When you came to OSS.'

'Just orientation.'

'You never went to "The Farm"?'

'No.'

'I expect that this assignment will be uncomplicated and brief. Once Alessa trusts you, her asset will turn over the name we need and that will be the end of it. But you should have some operational training. When do you see Alessa again?'

'Friday night.'

'It's Tuesday morning. That gives us time to send you up to "The Farm" for a couple of days. Make sure when you pack you include clothing for outdoor activities. When you come back to work on Friday we'll talk again.'

I didn't have time to get scared or nervous. Two hours later, after spinning my cover story to my girls and to Phoebe as I packed in my bedroom, I found myself standing on the Eleventh Street side of the Raleigh Hotel with my suitcase.

A black Ford coupé with bulging fenders and a Maryland license plate pulled over in front of me. The driver leaned out his window.

'I'm Jack,' he said, using the code name I'd been given.

I got into the car.

'From now on,' Jack said, 'you will use your first name only. Tell no one anything about yourself or your job. No exceptions.'

SIX

I struggled helplessly in the man's grip. He wasn't big or particularly strong, but he had me in a head and shoulder lock I couldn't escape. Pulled from behind off balance, I scrabbled for footing in the dead leaves and dirt.

The blade tip of the long knife touched my wrist, and I knew I was a dead woman.

'This is the radial artery,' Sergeant Smith said, loosening his chokehold on my neck. With relief bordering on euphoria I drew in a lungful of air. 'It's only a quarter inch below the surface of the skin, so it's a good spot for a girl to target. This artery's tiny, though, so slice right across the entire wrist as deep as you can so you make sure you get it. Your attacker will lose consciousness in about fourteen seconds and bleed to death in a minute and a half.'

I'd arrived at 'The Farm' in time for combat knife instruction. I'd joined Myrna and Sandy, the other women in my group, after changing into slacks, jacket, and canvas shoes.

Sergeant Smith released me. Even though I knew he was just demonstrating, I loathed the helplessness I felt in his grip. I was eager to learn how to defend against it.

'Now,' Sergeant Smith said, 'you girls, if you're attacked from the front, you're likely to be shorter than your assailant. We'll go more into hand-to-hand combat tomorrow, but your best bet is to shove your flat left hand under your attacker's chin as hard as you can and push him up and back, digging the fingers of that left hand into his eyes – no cringing, please. We call that grip the Tiger's Claw. That will force your attacker off balance and blind him. Once he's disabled, slash across the radial artery above his elbow. If you can't reach it, drop into a crouch and thrust up into his belly above the navel. You won't be able to penetrate the stomach artery with the knife we'll be issuing you, but you will be able to inflict some real damage and possibly escape.'

Smith held up the wicked looking knife – fifteen inches long at least, double-edged, with a deadly point – that he'd been using. 'This,' he said, 'is the Fairbairn-Sykes fighting knife. If you were men assigned to field-work, we'd give you one of these, but clearly–' and he grinned – 'this wouldn't fit into your handbags.'

He seemed disappointed that the three of us didn't laugh at his little joke.

'Here are your knives,' Smith said, handing us each a small cardboard box. I opened mine and found a pocketknife with a scored horn handle.

Smith pulled one like it from his pocket and held it up.

'This is a Schrade switchblade,' he said, 'developed for paratroopers, so they can cut their lines with one hand if they land tangled up in a tree. But it's an excellent small fighting knife because you only need one hand to use it.'

He demonstrated where to position the knife across our palms, how to manipulate the button that opened it, and then how to close and lock it.

When I pressed the tiny button on the knife's spine the blade shot out of the handle. It had a sharp point and one sharpened edge.

'Remember to keep your knife honed,' he said, 'otherwise you won't get a clean cut and the artery will close up and stop bleeding.'

The first time Sandy popped her blade open she squealed. She was a petite blonde with the JC Penney tag still hanging off her slacks. Myrna, an auburn-haired woman with long legs and a deep cleavage, was as gorgeous as a pin-up girl. She got comfortable with the knife's action quickly. Sandy needed a couple more demonstrations from

Sergeant Smith.

'Now I'll show you the basics of using the blade. Sandy,' Smith said, 'come over here. I'm going to pretend I'm coming at you. Don't open your blade, just show me what you'd do.'

'Holy smoke, Sergeant!' she said. 'Do I have to? I don't think I'll ever need to use a knife!'

'Don't comment on your assignment, Sandy. And this is basic training for females. You have to pass to go on to your assignment.'

'Oh,' she said. He came at her. 'Are we starting now?' she asked.

'Hesitation,' he said, 'might last forever. React, don't think. Louise, you try now.'

He came at me quickly, and as he reached for me I stopped his chin with my open left hand and forced his head back, then feinted with my closed knife across his upper arm.

'Very good!' he said. 'Now, Myrna.' He didn't move a half a step forward before she stopped him cold and slashed across his arm. 'Excellent!' he said.

'What if my attacker has a knife, too, or a revolver?' asked Sandy, her blue eyes so wide that I could see their whites.

'We'll show you some more hand-to-hand combat moves tomorrow,' he said. 'We're done for today. Get familiar with your knives. And there's reading material in your

63

rooms for you to go over tonight. Chow is in an hour in the dining room.'

The three of us hiked from the training field back up toward the country mansion that OSS dubbed 'The Farm'.

It sat on about a hundred acres of tobacco stubble and cattle pasture not far from Washington in southern Maryland. Soon after war was declared OSS had converted the house, barns, outbuildings, and polo grounds to training facilities for the Secret Intelligence Branch. The main house itself looked like an English manor. It had enough bedrooms to sleep over twenty trainees.

'The Farm' wasn't as military in its nature as the Special Operations training camps. Otherwise we'd be in tents and uniforms. Its curriculum was more informal, emphasizing observation, concealment, cover stories, bribery, how to handle agents, and such. I knew a few girls who'd already taken the truncated course for females here. My friend Joan Adams, who was one of Director Donovan's secretaries, was one.

I wouldn't say this out loud, but I was sick of living in the files and thrilled to be here! I doubted that getting one name from Alessa and delivering it to Max Corso would require any real spy type stuff, but I didn't care.

'That was jolly,' Myrna said as we trudged uphill, crunching through the frozen mud of

64

a farm road.

'I wouldn't say jolly,' I answered, 'but I liked learning to defend myself.'

'You two are all wet,' Sandy said. 'I'm sure I won't ever use this knife for anything other than cutting string. I hope not, anyway.'

True to the sergeant's word, we found a stack of reading material on each of the three single beds that lined one wall of the large room we'd share. The room was regal. It flaunted a stone fireplace, thick moldings, high ceilings, and oil paintings of the 'hunt and hound' sort crowding the walls.

Sandy sat on her bed cross-legged and hefted her stack of reading material, sighing. 'I really don't think I'm going to need all this,' she said, 'I'm only going to be—'

'Hush, Sandy,' I said. 'We're not supposed to talk about our assignments.'

'But we're alone!'

'Shut up, Sandy,' Myrna said. 'Or you will flunk out for sure.'

Sandy shut up, with a pout.

'Do you think we should dress for dinner?' I asked.

'Absolutely,' Myrna said. 'Never overlook the chance to make an impression.'

'Dibs on the bathroom,' Sandy said, collecting clothes and a toilet bag from her suitcase and heading down the hall.

Myrna stripped without bothering to turn her back to me. The woman had gorgeous undies. Her pale pink knickers edged with chocolate brown lace matched her bra, garter belt, and slip. She drew on silk stockings; where she found them these days I couldn't imagine.

I was more modest and turned my back to don my everyday white cotton underwear. No silk stockings for me – mine were rayon. I'd brought one dress with me, the simple black shirtwaist I'd worn to Bill's funeral years ago. I wore it seldom, so it was still like new, but I'd replaced the collar and cuffs with a contrasting plaid so the dress would look less funereal. I'd loved Bill very much, but he'd been dead for years now, and I was a different person.

When I turned back around Myrna was wearing a low-cut red jersey dress that clung to her hourglass figure and stacked heels that emphasized her long legs. She was a real dame, no question.

Sandy came into the bedroom wearing a blue sweater set and pearls that made her look like a schoolgirl.

I went down to the bathroom to put on my face. The only make-up I wore was powder and lipstick, even though, as Ada often remarked, I looked the thirty years old I was. I didn't see the point to foundation, since it seemed to slip right off my skin, and my glasses hid the thickest eye make-up I could apply.

Myrna sent Sandy and me downstairs ahead of her. 'I'll do my thing in the bath room and be down in a minute,' she said.

I found out why later when she made her entrance.

There were fifteen male trainees at 'The Farm' with us. Every one turned and gawked at Myrna when she walked into the dining room. I didn't blame them; I admired her looks too. The woman was so gorgeous that she reminded me of Rita Hayworth.

There were two large round tables in the dining room. Sandy and I had saved a seat for her at our table, but she swept right past us and sat down at the other, where she'd be the only woman.

Two colored boys in naval stewards' uniforms brought platters of pork chops, sweet potatoes, stewed apples, and rolls through the swinging doors of the kitchen. We were hungry from all that outdoor exercise and fell on the food like starving refugees.

After dessert and coffee one of the young men at our table, Harry from Topeka, turned to Sandy.

'One of the outbuildings here is tricked out like a cabaret,' he said. 'There's a juke box and three-two beer. Want to go over for a while?'

'Sure,' she said. 'If Louise comes with me.'

'I hope she does,' said the older man with a lovely British accent sitting next to me wearing tweed and, I swear, gaiters. 'I'm Sam,' he continued, offering me his arm.

After bundling up against the November cold we found ourselves at the door of what used to be a smokehouse, reading a home-made sign on the door – *Absolutely no alcoholic beverages will be sold to majors and colonels under twenty-one years of age unless accompanied by their parents* – which was an inside joke about the youth of our officer corps.

Once inside the door of the cabaret I was brought up short by a vulgar display on one of the walls. Humiliated would be an adequate word for how I felt, but I kept my embarrassment to myself. I knew I had to be a 'sport' to be accepted within OSS, no matter what unpleasantness I had to contend with. I'd be evaluated at the conclusion of my stay here at 'The Farm' and I intended to pass.

The wall in question was plastered with posters of half-naked pin-up girls draped over jeeps, airplanes, and tanks. A brunette clothed in panties, a bra, and a sailor's hat saluted a seaman on the deck of an aircraft carrier. Another luscious model in a bikini and heels rode astride a flying jet, long blonde hair flowing in the wind. The models' faces and figures were airbrushed and enhanced to the point they looked like cartoons instead of real women.

The government encouraged the display of

pin-up girls. Supposedly, they placated thousands of randy men in uniform and reminded them of what bliss waited for them at home after the war was won, but none of them resembled any living woman I knew.

But I kept my irritation to myself and accepted a beer from Sam. Someone put coins in the jukebox, and the Andrews Sisters' latest, 'Here Comes the Navy', filled the room with their usual close harmony. I checked the jukebox's contents. No hillbilly music. No Roy Acuff, no Carter family. I longed to hear a real country song, like Bob Wills' 'Dusty Skies', but I resigned myself to swing and crooning for the rest of the evening.

Then I marveled as Myrna took advantage of the shortage of girls – the very shortage that encouraged men to leer at pin-ups. The woman was a natural OSS 'glamour girl' already. She nursed one beer throughout the evening. Whenever she crossed her legs she left her skirt above her knee, and while talking to a man she tended to lean forward, revealing the tops of her breasts. She danced with every man there, even the young ones who could barely bring themselves to ask her, and played no favorites. But she stayed safely on the correct side of the sexy/slutty line. I wondered what sort of mission she was destined for. Perhaps she was one of those women who were willing to give all for their country.

Sandy and I had no shortage of dance partners either. I stuck to one beer too, but Sandy had several, and she turned out to be a giggler. When taps finally sounded, Myrna and I guided her back to our bedroom.

Going up the mansion's back stairs we came face-to-face with another pin-up on the landing. But this one was very different from the ones in the cabaret. It depicted a sweet-faced girl in a prim white shirt. The bold print ranged across the poster said: *She may look clean, but ...* The poster went on to warn men that pick-ups, good-time girls, and prostitutes carried syphilis and gonorrhea, and that soldiers and sailors couldn't fight the Axis if they had VD.

'Well,' Myrna said. 'Men. They don't know what to think of us, do they?'

After bathing and changing into pajamas we faced our stacks of reading material. In less than an hour Sandy dumped hers on the floor.

'I'll never need all this,' she said, turning off her bedside lamp and pulling her covers over her head.

I skimmed every document. I wanted to be more thorough, but there was too much to read carefully. The material covered observation, concealment, cover stories, bribery, communications, first aid, ciphers, and diagrams of weapons and unarmed combat.

When I fell sound asleep around midnight Myrna was still up reading and taking notes with a vengeance.

SEVEN

Reveille blared so loudly that it sounded like the trumpeter was sitting at the foot of my bed.

'Hell's Bells,' Myrna said, swinging her legs over the side of her bed.

I dragged myself upright. Sandy was already on her way to the bathroom, showing no signs of a hangover.

A knock sounded at our door. Without opening it Sergeant Smith hollered out to us, 'Calisthenics on the training ground, girls!'

We pulled on slacks and sweaters and went outside into the chilled air. It was still dark. Kerosene lanterns outlined a large rectangle in the dirt. A new instructor, Corporal Jones, organized us into three lines.

'Now you girls,' he said, placing us in the back row, 'we don't expect you to keep up with the men, just do your best.'

I sweated through jumping jacks and running in place, but the push-ups did me in. Myrna too. But I was pleased to see Sandy kept at it until after nearly half of the men had dropped out. At least one of us had exceeded the patronizing expectations of Jones.

After cleaning up we met again in the dining room. We downed waffles and eggs and even had orange juice. There was sugar for the coffee. I'd suspected the camp got extra rations; the orange juice and sugar proved it.

We were given fifteen minutes before meeting again in the classroom, which was set up in the long reception room of the mansion. At the door Smith beckoned to Sandy and pulled her aside.

The lights dimmed for a slide show on first aid, but Sandy didn't return to the room. I checked outside the door to see if she was sneaking a cigarette. No Sandy.

Smith leaned up against the wall.

'Where's Sandy?' I asked. 'Class is about to start.'

'Not coming,' Smith said.

'What? Where is she?'

'Gone.'

Back inside the room, in the dark punctuated by the shifting light of the changing slides, I passed a note to Myrna. She scanned it and raised an eyebrow. We both knew Sandy was booted for talking and drinking too much. Last night at the cabaret was what the OSS training curriculum referred to as a relaxation test, to see if one of us let down our guard under the 'influence of alcohol and social distractions'. Like vulgar pictures, attentive men, and booze. Sandy had flunked.

The morning passed slowly, while a medic named Brown, a lieutenant named Johnson and a red-headed civilian with an Irish accent named Miller lectured us on the topics already covered in our reading materials. Graphs, charts, and slide shows illustrated their points. Myrna nudged me once after I fell into a dead sleep.

Our studies outside of the classroom were more interesting. In the farmhouse's kitchen we learned how to steam open and reseal an envelope. Holding the envelope over a pot of smoking water, I learned to work my thumb ever so slowly under the envelope flap until it came loose. To my surprise, after the flap dried all I had to do to reseal it was lick the glue and stick the flap down. The envelope looked like it hadn't been tampered with at all.

The 'belongings test' was more challenging. I was led into a bedroom and shown an array of personal belongings laid out on the bed. I was allowed to study them for five minutes. Then I was required to list them and speculate about the individual who owned them. I couldn't remember all the items, but from the expression on the instructor's face I got the description of their owner more correct than not.

By noon we'd completed Spycraft 101.

After lunch Myrna and I found ourselves back outside on the training ground. The bracing air was a relief after being inside the house all morning.

Smith said nothing about Sandy's absence.

'OK, girls,' he said to us. 'Hand-to-hand combat. The first thing you need to remember is: size and strength have nothing to do with defending yourself.' He gestured to his head. 'It's all up here. Skill. And staying calm. To demonstrate, I brought along Private White here.'

Private White touched his cap.

'Usually, Private White dishes up our chow, and he's had no training other than the basics I'm going to show you. Watch what he can do.'

Smith slipped on an eye mask to protect his eyes from the 'Tiger's Claw'.

Then Smith charged White, who stopped him cold with the chin jab we learned yesterday. His left hand dug into Smith's eyes; Smith toppled over, and White dropped on him and pretended to ram his right knee into Smith's groin.

The two men climbed to their feet and dusted themselves off. Smith nodded to White, who left.

Smith put his hands on his hips. 'Girls,' he

said, 'this isn't about fighting fair. It's about killing or being killed. Now, this is a delicate subject, I understand, but immobilizing a man with a blow to his testicles is a fundamental technique of hand-to-hand combat, and it always works. You mustn't allow any reluctance about touching a man down there stop you from defending yourself. Of course, Private White didn't actually knee me, and you'll be relieved to know that you don't have to either.'

Myrna and I nodded with feminine humility, without daring to catch each other's eye.

'Myrna,' he said, 'you first.'

Smith donned his eye mask again and attacked her. Viciously. And exactly as he'd taught us, she stopped him cold with her flat hand under his chin, gouged at his eyes, dropped him to the ground, then pretended to shove her knee in his groin.

'Very good, Myrna, very good,' Smith said. 'Most girls are reluctant the first time they attack a man. Now you, Louise.'

Smith came at me, grasping my upper arms so hard that tears came to my eyes. I fought back, shoving my hand under his chin, forcing his head back, and gouging at his eyes. He dropped to the ground on his back, and in a moment of pure power, I shoved my right knee into his testicles as hard as I could.

Smith screamed and curled into a ball,

grabbing at his groin and flailing about on the ground. Men came running from all sides.

'It's all right,' Smith said, sitting up and gasping. 'It's OK. Louise got a little carried away, that's all.'

I knelt next to him. 'I'm so desperately sorry,' I said. 'I don't know what came over me.'

Smith gestured the other men away. They left, grinning.

'Really and truly,' I said, struggling to look contrite. 'I don't know what to say. I'm so embarrassed.'

'Forget it,' Smith said, still holding on to his equipment. 'These things happen.' I had to give the man credit. He handled the humiliation well.

Breathing hard, the sergeant got to his feet. 'Let's move on,' he said. 'We need to cover what to do if your assailant has a weapon – first a revolver, then a knife. A little less realism on your part would be appreciated, Louise.'

After our lesson Myrna and I climbed the hill from the parade ground to the farmhouse. We allowed ourselves a giggle.

'You know, Louise, there's more to you than first meets the eye,' Myrna said.

'You too,' I answered.

EIGHT

The taxi dropped me off at 'Two Trees' about supper time on Thursday night. Joe met me at the door with a finger to his lips. Despite the hour the dining room was empty.

'What's wrong?' I said.

'A huge naval battle has begun at Guadalcanal,' Joe said. 'The Japs are trying to retake the island. We know the *Enterprise* is involved.' Milt Junior was a signalman on the *Enterprise*, one of our biggest aircraft carriers. 'Phoebe is terribly upset. She's upstairs in her bedroom crying her eyes out. Dellaphine is with her.'

Another huge battle! How in God's name could the Allies manage to win a war spread out over entire continents and vast oceans? I felt like the world was being set on fire by demons and the Allies had a leaky hose to douse the flames. My knees felt a little weak, and Joe pulled me to him and held me tight.

'So much,' I said. 'All at once.'

'Yes, it is. But we'll get through it. And one person can only do so much.'

He was right. My job was to file endlessly at OSS and get a name from Alessa. I could do that. I could. I pulled myself together. Joe released me with a final squeeze.

'Poor Phoebe,' I said.

'I understand that she's distressed, but Milt's about as safe on the *Enterprise* as anyone can be in the Pacific. And Tom is far behind the lines, guarding a supply depot.'

Joe had no idea where most of his Czech friends and relatives were.

I pulled off my coat and hat. 'If Dellaphine is with Phoebe, what are we doing for dinner?'

'Henry is making pancakes. They should be about ready. And Madeleine found some maple syrup in a market on her way home from work.'

In the kitchen, Henry, with Madeleine's help, was dishing up stacks of fragrant pancakes.

'We turned off the radio,' Ada said. 'We couldn't listen any more.'

'It's like reading "Revelation",' Henry said.

Joe, Ada, Henry and I carried our plates into the dining room. Madeleine ate in the kitchen. None of us wanted to talk about the war any more, even Henry.

'So,' Ada said to me, 'can you tell us where you've been, what you've been doing?'

'Of course not. It was clerical and dusty.'

'Did you get to stay in a hotel? Did they

change the sheets and towels every day?'

'Yes and no. The food was good, though. Orange juice, plenty of coffee, pie for dessert.'

Henry groaned. 'God, that sounds wonderful,' he said.

We carried our plates back to the kitchen to find Madeleine had washed hers, left it on the drainboard, and gone down to the basement room she shared with her mother. She'd left the griddle and mixing bowl in the sink.

Henry exploded. 'That girl!' he said. 'Who does she think she is? She should be washing these dishes!'

'Why?' I said. 'Because she's colored? She's got a government job like we do. She washed her own dishes, didn't she? I'll finish up.'

'I'll dry,' Joe said, grabbing a kitchen towel from the rack.

Henry shook his head. 'What is going to happen to these Negroes when the war jobs go away, that's what I want to know? There's going to be trouble, that's what I think, putting these people back in their places.'

I expect Henry meant women too. Most of us were hired 'for the duration'.

I found Joan Adams, my dear friend and one of Director Donovan's secretaries, at Betty's typewriter when I arrived at work the next morning.

'What on earth are you doing here?' I said. 'Is everything OK?'

Joan pulled a sheaf of paper out of the typewriter with a gesture of finality.

'Betty's sick, and this one report had to be typed,' Joan said. 'It's not a problem, I had the time.'

'What's this about Betty?' I said to Ruth. Brenda wasn't in yet.

Ruth spoke without looking up from alphabetizing a stack of files.

'All I know is, Betty's room-mate called yesterday and said she was really sick. A high fever.'

'Not influenza, I hope.' That would be a disaster. Everyone in the office could come down with it.

'They didn't say. But we're doing OK. Things are pretty quiet for once. And Joan helped.'

'I'm not busy, Director Donovan's out of town.' Joan stood up and stretched her arms above her head. 'But I do need to get back to my own office.'

'Of course,' I said.

'Lunch?' Joan said.

'Absolutely.'

After Joan left, Ruth stopped her work and turned to me. 'Dr Murray wanted to see you in his office as soon as you came in,' she said, almost whispering. 'He said I wasn't to tell anyone but you.'

'Sure,' I said. 'I'm on my way.'

For appearances' sake I collected my note-book and pencil before walking down the hall to Don's office. He wasn't there. Platon Melinsky waited for me. He rose and pulled a chair up to the desk for me.

'So,' he said. 'How did it go at "The Farm"?'

'Fine, I think.'

'You passed without reservations. Congratulations, that's excellent work.'

'Thank you.'

Melinsky studied the glowing end of his cigarette stub, then ground it out in an ashtray. 'Tell me,' he said. 'Did you enjoy it?'

I hesitated.

'With all honesty, please. I need to know.'

'Yes, actually, I did.'

'In what way?'

'I liked learning to defend myself.'

Melinsky nodded. 'Good,' he said. 'I wanted to hear that. Remember, though, you took a very short course.'

'I understand, Mr...' I paused. What was I supposed to call him? Prince?

'I'm a Lieutenant Colonel in the US Army paratroopers, so Colonel Melinsky is fine.' He leaned across the desk. 'We need to talk about tonight, when you'll see Alessa again.'

Melinsky pulled a small envelope from his pocket and handed it to me. 'Give this to Alessa. It confirms that we are following her instructions to the letter. And don't be surprised if she doesn't give you anything in return tonight. Her asset will be waiting to see our *bona fides*.'

Melinsky unfolded an Esso tourist map of Washington and spread it out on the desk. Thank God for oil company road maps. For many countries, and parts of our own, they were the only maps available.

'Show me where you live, where you meet your knitting friends, all the details you can think of.'

'My rooming house is on I Street, here. The knitting circle meets here, at the Union Methodist Church, two blocks east and around the corner on Twentieth. We start about seven o'clock and work until around nine o'clock, and then we all go home. That's about it.'

Melinsky traced my route on the map with a finger. 'This is what I want you to do. After the circle breaks up, take your usual route home. But when you get to Twenty-First and I, cross the street to the filling station. Go inside and get a Coke from the freezer. There's a side door on the north side of the building. Our friend Jack will be waiting there to bring you to me. He'll be driving a different car tonight.'

'All right.'

Melinsky stood and extended his hand. 'Good luck,' he said.

I shook his hand. His grip was firm, almost painful from the pressure of his heavy gold signet ring.

The OSS cafeteria was packed, mostly with men in uniform. Not only American uniforms, either. I saw two Scottish Highland Regiment officers in Black Watch kilts and a clutch of Brits in peaked caps and Sam Browne belts.

Joan and I fought our way through the crowd to the cafeteria line, where we selected macaroni and cheese, canned peas, milk, and Waldorf salad with a cherry on top, all for sixty cents. We scraped the debris off an abandoned table and sat down.

'So,' Joan said. 'How was it?'

'What? Sorting postcards?'

'Please,' she said. '"The Farm". I know you went there.'

'I'm not supposed to talk about it.'

'For heaven's sake, we're on campus. And no one can hear us over this din.'

'It was OK.'

'When I was there I passed all the physical exercise tests. You know I'm taller than most men, and tennis has kept me fit. The lectures made me sleepy, though. And I never did learn how to steam open an envelope and reseal it. I passed with reservations.'

'Really.' I dug into my salad as if it were chocolate cake.

'Why did Don decide to send you to "The Farm" now?'

'He said because we had a lull in our workload.'

'He doesn't have a special assignment for you?'

'Like what? I'm a file clerk.'

'Want to come to my place tonight? We could have a couple of Martinis and dinner.'

'I would love to, but I can't. Knitting socks for our boys tonight.'

'Surely, you can skip it once.'

'I'd rather not.' I ran out of food to keep my mouth full and limit my responses.

'How about Saturday?'

'I'm going shopping with a friend.' Alessa might want me to meet her on Saturday again.

'OK, be a party-pooper.'

'Sorry.'

Back in my office I went behind the partition that separated my desk from the others to recover my poise. My closest friend had tested my ability to keep my mouth shut, and I'd passed. Melinsky must have recruited her. Thank God I'd realized she was pumping me. If I'd gone over to her apartment for Martinis she would have kept trying to break my resolve. I understood now that spies had no friends. I was glad I wasn't going to be one for long.

NINE

Alessa collected her knitting bag and coat while her mother-in-law frowned at her disapprovingly.

'Knitting is such an inappropriate occupation for you, dear,' she said. 'Surely, you can find something more appropriate to do.'

'I love to knit, *Madre*, you know that. And I can practice my English at the same time.'

'But the people you are associating with! Who are they?'

'Regular American women. I like them.'

Sebastian looked up from the stacks of paperwork and accounts he and Orazio were studying on the breakfast table.

'Leave her be, Mamma,' Sebastian said. 'Alessa can do as she pleases. Have fun, *cara*,' he said to her.

Alessa couldn't resist running over to Sebastian and kissing his mop of curly brown hair before leaving the apartment. Her husband, with his thick spectacles and poetic nature, was no warrior, but he was the kindest man she'd ever known. He must have inherited it from his father, because his mother was *una stronza*. Being married to Sebastian was worth living in the same apartment as her mother-in-law, Alessa reminded herself, and it wouldn't be forever.

At her locker in the sub-basement Alessa changed into her refugee disguise.

Sebastian couldn't fight in the war. The British, the Canadians, and the Americans had all rejected him because of his poor vision. But Turi had asked Alessa to do more than knit socks, and she intended to do it, no matter how dangerous it was.

TEN

It seemed even colder in the basement of the Union Methodist Church women's club room than it was outside. The church turned off its central heating during the week, so the six of us crowded our chairs around an old-fashioned tubby coal furnace. The sexton was kind enough to leave us a scuttle of coal every week. It was still chilly enough for us to keep our coats on though.

Alessa wore her thrift shop greatcoat, as usual, and I had on my serviceable wool. I longed for a new coat with a real fur collar, but seeing Alessa in her threadbare clothes made me feel ashamed.

Four other women joined us tonight. Two of them stayed warm in full-length furs. The others were ordinary housewives bundled up in cloth coats like mine. But we were all here, in this freezing church basement, to do something, anything, to help win the war. In my case I did it badly, I'm afraid.

'Ladies,' one of the housewives, Laura, said, 'I found this great pattern in *Ladies' Home Journal*, for fingerless gloves. I wrote a copy out for each of us.'

'This is wonderful,' one of the mink clad women, Pearl, said. 'The soldiers love these. Keeps their hands warm but their fingers free to do their work. Thanks.'

I inspected the glove pattern. No way would I ever be able to knit it. When I looked up I saw Alessa grinning at me.

'Go ahead, laugh,' I said.

'As I mentioned the last time we talked, I'm sure you have other abilities.'

The other women giggled. When I looked hurt, Pearl put her hand on my arm. 'Listen,' she said, 'you're working at a real government job, so you don't have much time to practice.'

We dutifully pulled our projects out of our knitting bags and got to work. I took advantage of the moment to give Alessa an envelope containing the OSS's answer to Turi's note agreeing with all his, and Alessa's, instructions.

'Here are directions to that consignment shop you wanted to visit,' I said to Alessa. When our hands touched she squeezed my fingers and our eyes met. For a second we saw deep into each other's soul. She was a fine person, and I regretted we'd need to break off our friendship when our mutual foray into espionage was over.

So we knitted. And knitted. The fingers of some of these women – including Alessa's –

flew. I labored along, but had to ask Alessa for help with a dropped stitch only once.

No one asked Alessa why she wore a man's used coat, or what the other women's husbands did for a living. We worked and talked about how coffee would be rationed at the end of November and the rumors that new ration books for even more foodstuffs would be issued after Christmas.

'Frankly, I'm glad they're going to ration coffee,' I said. 'Then everyone will have their fair share without needing to queue up at the grocery stores.' Dellaphine queued once a week to buy groceries in short supply, but some people simply didn't have the time.

'I bought some margarine this week,' Laura said.

'Really?' Pearl said. 'Was it awful?'

'Not if you're out of butter.'

'But it's such an ugly white color,' I said.

'It came with yellow food coloring,' Laura said. 'My children got a kick out of mixing it in.'

'I've had margarine too,' Alessa said. 'It tastes best when you spread it on something hot.'

At the end of our two hours we packed up our knitting bags, wrapped scarves around our heads, and pulled on our gloves.

Alessa hung back, and I stayed behind with her.

'I almost forgot,' she said. 'I found a new

90

pattern for you too. Don't make that face, it's easy. It's a sock pattern without a heel.'

'No heel?'

'It's like a tube. So you don't have to turn a heel. And it fits all sizes.'

She handed me a folded paper, and I could feel the small envelope hidden inside it. I was surprised; Melinsky had told me to expect nothing from her tonight.

'Thanks,' I said, stuffing it into my coat pocket. 'Listen, would you like to have lunch again tomorrow? Maybe we can go to a movie?'

She shook her head. 'Can't,' she said. 'My cousin has loaded me up with chores. Some other time. But I'll see you here next week.'

'OK,' I said. I had a sudden urge to throw my arms around her and hold her close, which I managed to suppress. I was beginning to think of this woman as a friend, someone I cared about, and I shouldn't do that.

I did exactly as Platon instructed me, walking across the street to the filling station instead of going straight home. I leaned over the bright-red chest freezer and pulled out a freezing cold Coca Cola. After popping the cap on the bottle opener on the side of the freezer, I took a long, sweet swallow. The Coca Cola Company had convinced the government not to restrict their sugar allotment, as their product was essential to the morale of the war effort. I agreed.

I strolled out the side door of the filling station, and sure enough, there was Jack waiting for me behind the wheel of an old Ford woody with a rusted out running-board. He didn't speak to me, but tipped his fedora. We drove north a block, then turned on K and headed east. I didn't ask him where we were going. Some café or other, I guessed.

Four blocks later we turned on to Connecticut Avenue, where the glamorous May-flower Hotel reigned over what Washing-tonians called the 'Fifth Avenue of DC'. I'd been inside several times, since Joan rented her studio apartment there. To my surprise Jack pulled over in front of the equally famous restaurant two doors down.

'We're here,' Jack said.

'Jack, this is Harvey's!'

'Yes, ma'am. The first floor is a public bar and restaurant for men. When you go inside, you need to take the staircase on your right up to the second floor. Tell the maître d' that you're joining Colonel Melinsky, and they'll show you to his table.'

'I'm not dressed properly!' And I would have to carry my knitting bag with me!

'There's a war on, ma'am. No one will care.'

I stood on the sidewalk and took in the iron front facade of the legendary restaurant, its wood-framed entrance and signature glowing blue neon sign. I collected myself. Why shouldn't a telegrapher's widow from Wilmington, North Carolina have dinner with a Russian prince at Harvey's? Anything seemed possible during this war.

I climbed the stairs and presented myself at the maître d's desk as if I took my knitting bag with me to every fine restaurant in town. He led me to the very back of the wood-paneled room to a corner table, where Melinsky rose to greet me.

'Mrs Pearlie, thank you for joining me.'

'Thank you for asking me, Colonel,' I said. Melinsky wore the uniform of an Army colonel with the addition of a red-lettered Army Airborne patch on his left sleeve.

The waiter seated me, spreading a napkin in my lap, a new experience for me, and presented me with a menu. When I saw the menu items, my head reeled.

Melinsky smiled at me. 'This is why I wore my uniform. Soldiers get special menus here. Roosevelt's orders, so us fighting men can get a good meal. Would you like a drink? And order whatever you want to eat, please.'

I'd craved a Martini for a week. I'd gobbled down a cream cheese and pickle sandwich before I left for the knitting circle, but I was already hungry. I wasn't sure what to do.

Melinsky noticed my hesitation. 'Remember what I said at our first meeting? I am the only person you can behave naturally with, discuss anything with.'

'I'll have a Martini, no olive,' I said to the hovering waiter.

'Vodka, neat,' Melinsky said. 'And a dozen oysters each to start, please.'

The drinks arrived. I sipped on my Martini. Its cool smoothness slid down my throat. I'd never had a cocktail before I came to Washington. My grandparents, all four of them strict Southern Baptists, would turn over in their graves if they knew.

Melinsky shook pepper on his vodka, tossed it back in one gulp, and gestured for another one.

'I never had a drink until I came here,' I said. 'My family is southern Baptist. If they knew half of what I'd done since I arrived in the last year, well, I believe they'd change their name and leave Wilmington in disgrace.'

'What will you do after the war, then?'

'I don't know, but I assure you I'm not going home.'

The oysters arrived. These were not my parents' oysters. Not cornmeal battered and deep-fried like the ones I was used to cooking at my parents' fish camp, but slightly steamed, with melted butter and lemon on the side. I slid one succulent oyster down my throat, then another. When we were finished, Melinsky drained his second shot glass of vodka in one gulp.

'The taste of vodka reminds me I'm still Russian,' he said, beckoning for another.

'How long has it been since you've been home?' I asked.

'Nineteen-eighteen.'

'So many years!'

'Too many. But Stalin won't live forever, and I hope I can return one day before I die. I'm not a Romanov, and I have a British passport, so perhaps it may be possible.'

Much as I didn't want to find myself back in my hometown after the war, I found it hard to comprehend being banished from it forever.

The waiter returned to bring Melinsky another shot of vodka, clear off our oyster plates, and take our orders.

'Prime rib?' Melinsky asked me.

'Yes, please!' I'd never had prime rib before.

'Lobster thermidor for me, and another Martini for the lady,' Melinsky added.

After the waiter left Melinsky lowered his voice and leaned toward me. 'How went the knitting?'

I drew Alessa's papers from my knitting bag and handed them to him.

'This is a surprise,' Melinsky said, unfolding them. He smiled and handed me back the tube sock pattern. 'This is yours, I think.'

He opened the envelope and read the letter

it contained. It seemed quite short. Pensively, he tucked it into a uniform pocket. I couldn't read his expression, and just then the waiter brought us our plates.

The prime rib was wonderful. I ate every bite and all of the asparagus with hollandaise that accompanied it. One more Martini and I would have gnawed on the bone. I ignored the duchesse potatoes. Potatoes I could eat any time.

'That was wonderful, thank you,' I said.

'You are more than welcome,' Melinsky answered. I wondered if he was going to tell me anything about the letter's contents.

The waiter cleared away our plates and brought us coffee. With cream and sugar!

'I'm sorry to say,' Melinsky said, after the waiter left, 'that there were no names in Alessa's note. Some good information, but no names.'

I felt a stab of disappointment. When would Alessa deliver us the take, spy lingo for any information gathered by espionage? Before the slow convoys left, please!

'Did the two of you make any plans for the weekend?' he asked.

'No, she said she had too many chores to do, that she'd see me again at the next knitting circle.' An entire week from now.

'I think Alessa and her asset are still testing us,' Melinsky said, stirring his coffee in a slow circle. 'He's not going to give his information to her until he is sure he is safe.'

'So what next?' I asked.

'We must hope that by next week she collects the information we need and delivers it to you. That's all we can do.'

I turned my key in the lock of 'Two Trees' around eleven and found a reception committee waiting for me. Joe, Phoebe, and Ada erupted from the lounge and circled me.

'Where have you been?' Phoebe asked. 'We've been worried sick.'

Of course. I should have been home hours ago.

'I'm so sorry! I didn't mean to worry you. Some of the girls and I went out for a beer and a sandwich.' I was learning to lie without batting an eyelash.

'The café didn't have a telephone?' Joe asked, quietly taking my coat and hanging it on the coat rack. Joe was upset, I could tell from the tight line of his lips and the creases in his forehead.

'I'm so sorry,' I said again. 'I didn't think.'

'Obviously not,' Joe said.

'Give us a jingle, honey, the next time you stay out,' Ada said. 'Or let us know that you might be late before you leave.' Talk about the pot calling the kettle black.

Ada partied at all hours. We never knew where she was, except that she was dancing and drinking somewhere. Ada could be counted on to be late. Me, I guess I was the dependable sort everyone panicked about if I didn't get home at nine o'clock on the dot.

Phoebe and Ada went on upstairs to bed, leaving Joe and me alone, but not really alone. If only one of us could afford an apartment! He reached his arms around me and buried his face in my neck. A cascade of pleasure flooded my body.

'I was worried about you,' he said, his voice muffled by my shoulder.

'I'm sorry,' I said for the third time. 'But I am a grown woman, you know. Too old for a curfew,' I continued, teasing him. 'No one has to wait up for me.'

'You're not just any woman to me.' And he kissed me, sending more tremors throughout my body. 'We must do something about this, love,' he said. We both knew that a hotel room, even one out of town, was out of the question. We could pretend to be married, but if the desk manager questioned us at all we could be arrested, and it would ruin my career. Not Joe's; men were expected to do such things.

'Some day, one of our friends with an apartment will go out of town and lend us their place,' Joe said. 'We have to wait until then.'

Later, under my blankets and on the edge of sleep, I wondered why neither of us had discussed marriage. That was the normal way of things between single people. You got married to have sex. The truth was, I didn't want to marry Joe. He didn't have two nickels to rub together, and I knew too little about him to marry him. I wanted to have an affair with him. A year ago such a thought would have set me to praying for my soul during church. Today I felt frustrated and unhappy.

ELEVEN

What better way to put Alessa and Joe out of my mind than to start on the ground floor of Woodies, among the two-story cast iron arches and gleaming walnut counters, and work my way up to the Tea Room on the seventh floor?

Woodward and Lothrop department store occupied an entire block, between Tenth, Eleventh, F and G Streets, a few blocks east of the White House.

By the time I'd reached the fourth floor, I'd bought two pairs of rayon stockings, *Black Orchids* by Rex Stout, and a set of undies like Myrna's, except I chose soft blue with black lace trimming.

The weather was growing colder, and I'd need much warmer clothes than I'd brought with me from North Carolina. Fuel oil was scarce, and the government decreed that bedrooms should remain unheated during the coming winter. I'd already ordered the basics from the Sears catalog. When Ada'd found me at the dining room table filling out the order form she'd had a conniption. 'How do you expect to find a man wearing those?' she'd asked, looking in horror at the wide-legged wool trousers I was ordering in brown and olive.

'I'm not looking for a man,' I'd said. 'I'm looking to stay warm.'

I did want at least one purchase a bit more special than Sears' trousers, and I found it in Ladies' Dresses, an autumn-green wool suit dress for $12.95. The thought of wearing my new undies under it gave me a frisson of pleasure.

Shoes were scheduled to be rationed after Christmas, so I wanted a pair of tough saddle shoes, but I'd get a better deal on those at Hahn's.

Then I came upon the Fur Salon. The Woodies' ad in this morning's paper offered wool coats with mink collars for ninety-eight dollars, which I couldn't possibly afford, but no one could stop me from trying one on, could they?

The least expensive coats hung inside the entrance to the Fur Salon. I put down my packages and began to flip through them. Did I want blue, brown, or black? Blue, I decided as I pulled a coat off the rack. Dropping my own coat, which I'd purchased when Bill and I married years ago, to the floor, I drew on the new one. The fur collar nestled luxuriously around my neck. I turned, searching for a full-length mirror. I looked deeper into the long salon, where an older woman, gray-haired, dripping with bracelets and rings, modeled a breathtaking sheared beaver greatcoat. A young woman wearing a calf-length mink, with another fur coat draped over her arm, was with her. When the younger woman reached out to adjust her companion's collar I saw she wore a wide gold bracelet and a wedding band encrusted with diamonds.

Something intuitive made me duck behind a pillar before I consciously understood why. The young woman turned to beckon for a salesgirl. It was Alessa.

Shock forced heat into my face, and my heart missed a beat. Several beats. How could this be possible? Alessa was a poor refugee. The woman I saw was wealthy and aristocratic in her looks and bearing.

My legs wobbled like jelly, and I felt like I was floating in the air. I recognized the signs of a fainting spell, but I forced my back against the pillar hard. I used both hands to squeeze the back of my neck and the stars receded. Thank God.

I must have absorbed some of my lessons from 'The Farm', because despite my shock I didn't step out from behind my pillar to gape at the two women. Instead I stayed behind the pillar and watched the Fur Salon exits so I could see the two women when they left.

Then I heard her voice, answering the older woman's Italian – or maybe it was Sicilian – in familiar accented English. It was Alessa, there was no doubt about it. The two women passed by my pillar hideout on their way out of the Salon.

I knew I shouldn't follow her; I didn't have enough training to tail her expertly, and if she spotted me it would ruin the operation. Still trembling, I hung up the fur-collared coat I hadn't even admired myself in and collected my parcels.

I assumed my best gossipy expression and located the saleswoman who'd waited on them. She was hanging up the gorgeous coat Alessa's older companion tried on. 'Those ladies,' I said to her. 'I can't help wondering who they were. They wore such wonderful clothes and jewels.'

The saleswoman was miffed that they hadn't bought the coat, because she broke a famous Woodies' rule and answered me.

'That is the Dowager Countess Lucia Oneto and her daughter-in-law, Alessa. They are Italians or something. Very rich.' She continued tidying up the rack of furs. 'Would you believe,' she said, 'the daughter-in-law talked the Countess out of buying that coat? Said she should buy war bonds instead.'

I couldn't tell if the saleswoman admired Alessa or if she was angry to lose a sale.

Probably, a little of both.

'Do you know where they live?' I asked.

'I've said too much already,' the sales-woman said. 'I could get fired.'

I took the elevator up to the Tea Room to settle my nerves and think of what to do next. The menu was reduced from its usual extravagance because of the war, but I ordered a cup of tea and a slice of honey cake.

By the time I'd finished my tea my shock had subsided. Random questions raced through my mind. Why was Alessa posing as a poor refugee when she was a Sicilian countess? Was her husband, the supposed count, alive and in this country? Was the Oneto family important? Were they involved in Alessa's plan, or ignorant of it? Who was Alessa's asset? He must be involved somehow in the Port of New York, but Alessa lived here in Washington. How did they communicate?

My only task, during my brief stint as an OSS agent, was to get the name of the Mafia sleeper Alessa said her asset possessed before the next slow convoy left New York Harbor for Casablanca. That was it. No matter who Alessa was, no matter who her asset was. OSS would want nothing to interfere with this operation. I certainly could do nothing about what I'd discovered today until I briefed Melinsky on Monday.

That left the rest of the weekend for me to brood about why Countess Alessa Oneto disguised herself in thrift store clothing. She kept secrets, of course, everyone in this city did, but I had become fond of her. I knew I shouldn't have. It was unprofessional. I needed to think of her only as an asset, nothing more.

At least I'd be distracted tonight. Joe and I were going on our second official date. I'd made the plans this time. Joe had never been to an American movie, so we were going to see *Holiday Inn*, and then out to eat somewhere cheap, like Scholl's or Childs. He was poor as a church mouse, and I didn't want to embarrass him.

TWELVE

It was growing dark outside when Joe and I left the movie theater.

'What did you think?' I asked Joe.

'Well,' he said, wrinkling his forehead with puzzlement. 'It was entertaining. And the music was catchy. Bing Crosby has a good voice for a popular singer. The dancing was remarkable; I've never seen anything like it. No wonder Crosby and Fred Astaire are such big stars.'

We walked aimlessly down the street holding hands. I wore my new suit and undies, and felt young and attractive, despite having turned thirty.

'Look,' Joe said, pointing at a pub across the street. 'Let's see if they're serving dinner.'

We jaywalked across the street and discovered the pub had British pretensions, with a sign hanging over the door identifying it as 'The St George'. A fierce red dragon in neon and a Guinness logo graced the window, whatever Guinness was.

'I wonder if they really have Guinness here.

I'd love a pint,' Joe said.

'What is it?'

'A heavy stout. Very heavy, almost black in color. Definitely an acquired taste.'

We went into the pub, which was suitably dark with paneled wood walls and leather booths. A young waitress seated us and then gave Joe the bad news with the menu.

'No Guinness, I'm afraid, not until the end of the war. Awful, it is. I keep telling my boss he should scrape the sign off the window – so many Brits come in here hoping and are so disappointed – but he won't. Says it brings in custom.'

We settled for two Schlitzes. Joe ordered fish and chips, and I requested cottage pie.

'So,' I said as we sipped our beers and waited for dinner, 'except for the music and dancing, you didn't think much of the movie?'

'It was so silly. The Washington's Birthday sequence was ridiculous.'

'I think that's the idea. Aren't the newsreels realistic enough for you?'

'Good point. And I have a feeling we'll be hearing that Christmas song again, what was the title?'

'White Christmas.'

Our food arrived and was quite tasty. My cottage pie was made with lamb rather than beef. I'd eaten lamb a few times since I'd come to Washington, and I rather liked the flavor. To my surprise Joe shook malt vinegar all over his French fries, or as the British called them, chips.

'This brings back memories. I lived on fish and chips at university,' he said.

'Where did you go?' I asked, without thinking. Joe spoke little about his past, protecting his identity, from what threats I didn't know and didn't ask. 'Oh, I'm sorry, never mind!'

'It's fine. I went to Cambridge. Those were great years. Not a care in the world. I read English literature. I thought if I could live in Prague and teach English at one of the universities my life would be perfect.'

'Did you have rooms in college and row and everything?'

'It's scull, not row, darling, and yes, all of it, even the scholar's robe.'

He'd called me darling!

Unaware that he'd made my evening, Joe called for the check.

'Do you remember where we left Phoebe's car?' he asked.

'It's a couple of blocks down,' I said.

On our way, walking hand in hand, Joe stopped and scouted the street. 'Come on,' he said, pulling me through a tiny wrought iron gate into a wooded park no bigger than half a city block. The oaks and maples were bare of leaves, but we found a bench mostly hidden by the trunk and lower branches of a thick cedar tree. Joe sat and reached for me, pulling me on to his lap and into his arms. He spread his legs slightly so I could be even closer to him, and he kissed me. It was dark and chilly, but I was warm in short order. We kissed hard and deeply; his hand found its way inside my suit jacket and caressed my breast in its pretty bra. I responded by reaching deep under his belt and trousers and down his back.

'Is it too cold?' he asked.

'Never,' I answered.

A beam of blinding light flashed in our faces and drove us apart.

'It's a good thing I got here when I did,' the DC auxiliary policeman said. He was heavy, huffing and puffing in the long black coat and wide yellow armband that identified him. He was armed with a flashlight, truncheon, and a whistle on a lanyard. 'In five more minutes I would have arrested you for public fornication.'

Joe pulled himself together first. 'I assure you, officer—' he began.

'Holy smoke,' the policeman interrupted, angling the flashlight beam so he could see us. 'You should be ashamed, at your age. I figured you were some GI and his girl. You two should know better than to make a spectacle of yourselves like this.'

He poked at Joe with his truncheon. Joe clenched his fists, but he kept his temper.

'You two move along now,' the ersatz cop said. 'You don't want me to arrest you and get your pictures in the newspaper. That would embarrass the young lady.'

'We're on our way,' Joe said, through gritted teeth.

'Thank you, officer,' I said to him, in my most contrite voice. 'It won't happen again.'

We didn't speak until we found ourselves in Phoebe's car.

'Bloody hell!' Joe said, striking the steering wheel with both flat palms. He turned to me. 'I'm sorry, darling. I shouldn't have put you in such a position.'

I had to snicker.

'It's funny now,' Joe said. 'But what if we'd been arrested!'

I stopped laughing and shivered. I would have lost my job, Phoebe would evict me, and I'd have to crawl back home to my parents' house, ruined, as the preachers said. Joe wouldn't suffer as much. It wasn't fair.

We pulled into Phoebe's driveway near to midnight.

Her bedroom light was on.

'Someone suffers from insomnia in this house every damn night,' Joe said. He turned to me. 'Are you OK?'

'I'm fine. Don't worry about me. No necking in public parks in the future, I suppose.'

'And little enough in private.'

★ ★ ★

110

Exhausted, I climbed into my bed. Dellaphine had added an extra blanket because of the fuel oil restrictions, and I wore one of my new flannel pajama sets, the one with purple stripes and pink flowers. I tried not to think about Joe and our lack of privacy; it was too frustrating. How could we possibly have an affair while living in a boarding house? No wonder couples lined up around the block at the DC courthouse to get married. At least then they could share a bedroom without scandal.

I didn't want to get married anytime soon; I wanted an exciting romance with Joe. Oh, the hell with it! We'd never have any private time together unless one of us could get an apartment! A hotel room was just too risky.

By forcing myself not to think of Joe, my mind instantly returned to Alessa. The coincidence of encountering her in the Fur Salon flabbergasted me. Such a close call! If she'd seen me I suppose the entire OSS operation would have fallen apart.

More secrets, more cover stories; Washington was thick with them. Joe had them, Ada had them, Melinsky had them. Alessa's was just one more.

THIRTEEN

The porter silently cleared the dinner dishes off the small table in the breakfast room and piled them on his cart. Lina, the maid, brought hers in from the kitchen – her head lowered, as if she was committing an indiscretion – to add to the porter's cart. Orazio held the apartment door open so the porter could manhandle his cart into the hotel hallway.

Lina went back into the kitchen to brew the after-dinner tea. Alessa would have given anything for coffee, but they could only buy enough for breakfast.

The four of them, Alessa, Sebastian, Lucia, and Orazio, assumed their usual after-dinner seats in the living room of the apartment. Lucia and Alessa relaxed on the brocaded sofa, while Orazio and Sebastian took the leather wing chairs. Alessa knew how Lucia hated Orazio spending the evening with them. She'd said so often enough that both Alessa and Sebastian feared Orazio had overheard her.

Although Orazio Rossi was a *signore* with a

respectable surname, and a graduate of the University of Salerno, he was still an employee, Sebastian's trusted secretary. Sebastian insisted to his mother that Orazio live as they did. What was Orazio supposed to do, Sebastian said, stay in his bedroom? Alessa was glad of Orazio's company for Sebastian. He was young and well educated. They spent much of their time together keeping track of the Oneto fortune, which Sebastian's father had wisely stashed in Switzerland and New York long before Mussolini had overpowered Sicily.

Money was another of Lucia's complaints. The Onetos lived frugally so Sebastian could contribute to a number of war charities. He refused to lease a larger apartment or a house, even if they could have located one. He cut their allowances. Alessa had overheard son and mother arguing only yesterday. 'I can't fight, but I will contribute every *lira* I can to winning this war,' Sebastian said. 'You'll have to get used to it.'

Alessa thought of her own ongoing contribution to the war, her mission for Turi, her cover identity, and felt a tingle of excitement. At last there was something important she could contribute! She was so bored with sitting around the apartment. She wasn't afraid; what was there to be afraid of? Louise had no idea who Alessa really was. Turi would give her the *Mafioso* sleeper's name,

113

she'd deliver it to Louise, and that would be the end of it. She wished she and Louise could remain friends, but Turi insisted she must cut Louise off once Alessa delivered his final message to the OSS. Alessa liked Louise enough to keep wearing that awful greatcoat, the one she'd bought at the thrift store near Union Station.

Lina brought in the tea tray and set it on the dining table. She knew how everyone wanted theirs – Lucia's with milk and honey, Alessa's with honey only, and the men's black. Lina was nearly fifty years old and had worked for the Oneto family all her life, though she spoke some English thanks to informal lessons from Sebastian's British tutor. She was the only servant the Onetos had been able to bring with them. Alessa thought she must be very lonely.

Lina had a tiny room and bath off the kitchenette. She took her meals on a tray in her bedroom, then delivered her dishes to the porter. Lina and Alessa fixed breakfast for the family every morning and tea in the afternoon. Bread, eggs, cereal, and milk were still plentiful in the market, and it saved them a little money.

'You have no business cooking; it's beneath you,' Lucia said to her at least once a week. 'And all that knitting! Knitting is for *donne agricole anziane!*'

'I enjoy both very much, *Madre*,' Alessa

would answer. 'And I need to stay busy.'

In Sicily the Oneto family owned two houses: one in Palermo, and one in the country. Both held more than enough sitting rooms, libraries, bedrooms, and bathrooms for everyone to have all the privacy they needed. Most of the time Lucia lived in the town house, while Sebastian and Alessa preferred the country. The green and hilly country, aromatic with lemon and olive trees, how Alessa longed for it!

Here the four of them and Lina squeezed into what the hotel called a semi-house-keeping apartment with three bedrooms, two bathrooms, a kitchenette, a dinette, a maid's room, and a living room with a picture window that overlooked Connecticut Avenue. Of course, she and Sebastian shared a bedroom; Orazio used the smallest of the three bedrooms, and Lucia the other. Alessa and Lucia shared one bathroom, Orazio and Sebastian the second, and Lina used her own tiny washroom. This was one reason Alessa and Sebastian had postponed having children. Where would they put an infant and a nursemaid?

'Darling,' Alessa said, before Sebastian had a chance to immerse himself in *The Italian Tribune*, 'would you mind if I went to New York for a few days next week? My friend from school, Anna Bruno, you met her the last time we were in the city, has asked me to

115

visit. Her husband is overseas, you know.'

'Of course I don't mind,' her husband answered. 'Go. Have fun.'

Alessa thought her husband was the sweetest man in the world, really.

'How will you travel, my dear?' Lucia asked. 'Not on the train!'

'Of course on the train,' Alessa said.

'But it is so crowded! With soldiers, and there are no more first-class cabins!'

'So one must travel with the lower classes, such a hardship,' Orazio said.

Lucia shot him an irritated glance, unsure if he was criticizing her.

'Darling,' Sebastian said. 'I didn't consider the train. Are you sure it's safe?'

'Of course! It will be full of American soldiers! How much safer could it be? Besides, I like practicing my English, talking to regular Americans. They're so, sort of, simple and genuine.'

'Unlike us jaded Europeans, who've seen many more wars fought by the people who didn't start them,' Orazio said.

'You haven't given up your socialist leanings then, Orazio,' Sebastian said, not uncritically.

'Those terrible people!' Lucia said.

'The world will be different after the war is over, Mamma, we might as well be prepared.'

'But not for socialism! Mussolini would be

116

better than that!'

'Mussolini will be hung by the Italian people as soon as they can get at him,' Orazio said.

Lucia was aghast. 'But then what will happen?'

'Calm yourself, Mamma,' Sebastian said. 'Whatever government rules Italy, we will return to our home in Sicily, and I expect life there will go on much as before.'

Orazio said nothing more.

FOURTEEN

'Betty's not still out sick?' I asked. 'How long has it been now?'

'Since the day you left last week,' Brenda answered, while bandaging her scissoring hand. 'One of her room-mates called this morning. Ruth talked to her.'

Ruth stretched at her desk. Files that needed to be alphabetized piled around her. 'I didn't get her name, but she said Betty was a little better. I wanted to talk to Betty myself, but the room-mate said she was asleep.'

This wasn't good news. This was the fifth workday Betty missed. I wondered if she was terribly ill or if something more serious was going on.

Then Don appeared at the office door, summoning me to my meeting with Colonel Melinsky. He escorted me to his office, then left the two of us together.

Melinsky wasn't prepared for what I told him.

'I don't want to insult you by asking you if you're sure,' he said. 'But are you sure?'

'Absolutely. It was Alessa. In a mink coat

118

and expensive jewelry. The salesgirl told me she's a countess, Alessa Oneto. Her mother-in-law's name is Lucia.'

'My God,' Melinsky said, 'this puts a new twist on things. You didn't follow her, I hope.'

I shook my head. 'No,' I said, 'I was afraid they'd spot me.'

'Good work. *Merde*! Let me think for a minute.' He lit a cigarette and smoked it down to his fingers before he squashed it into an ashtray.

'This is surprising, but it really changes little,' he said.

'That's what I thought also.'

'Alessa disguised herself to avoid the attention you, and we, might have given her if we knew she was a countess. Almost like adding an additional cut-out between her asset and us. Quite clever, really.'

'Colonel, isn't it possible she assumed the disguise for our knitting group in the beginning? So we'd treat her as an equal? And it was only later that her asset approached her? She'd guessed I was a government girl.'

'Good point. That's very likely. So she had a disguise ready made and a contact – you – already.'

'Perhaps her family doesn't know about any of this?'

'Also possible. I will check the Onetos out, very subtly. I don't want them to get wind of this. When do you see Alessa again?'

'So far as I know, Friday night.'

'Does she have your telephone number?'

'I don't think so. I've never given it to her. And the listing is in my landlady's name.'

'Let's plan to meet again here, on Thursday, unless she's contacted you or I find out something pertinent about her background. Until then we go on as before.'

I went back to my office and found the Oneto family file I'd already retrieved and read. I'd return it immediately to its slot in the 'ON' file cabinet on the third floor, where Melinsky's secretary could find it when he requested it. Melinsky might be smart, educated, and accomplished, but he still thought like a man. It wouldn't have occurred to him that I'd take advantage of my job to find out whatever I could about Alessa and the Onetos on my own.

If Count Sebastian Oneto hadn't tried to enlist in the United States Army there would not be much information on him at all. He was rejected because of poor vision and a heart murmur, but the FBI had performed a background check on him, as they did on all foreign nationals who tried to enlist in the American military.

The Oneto family had fled Sicily when the Nazis arrived to build air bases. They'd lived in a hotel in London briefly while Sebastian attempted to enlist in the British Army.

When he was rejected, the family came to the United States. Their entry papers listed Sebastian; his wife, Alessa; his mother, Lucia; a maid, Lina; and the Count's personal secretary, Orazio Rossi. The Onetos had money, most of it socked away in Switzerland and New York City by Sebastian's late father. The family owned the usual olive groves and such in Sicily, but their real wealth stemmed from a profitable complex of sulfur mines. The family's address at a New York hotel was described as temporary. At some point they'd moved to Washington.

Orazio Rossi rated a brief paragraph. He and Sebastian had attended the University of Salerno together and become friends. Sebastian had studied Italian literature, Rossi law and history. Sebastian had hired him as his personal secretary after Sebastian's father's death. Louise found it irritating that the author of Rossi's FBI profile dwelled on Orazio's political activities while he was at the university. He made much of Orazio's membership in a student organization affiliated with the PSI, the outlawed Italian Socialist Party. So what, Louise thought. What intelligent university student worth his salt wouldn't be flirting with socialism while living in a country ruled by a vicious fascist dictator? Really, the FBI often seemed to forget that the United States was fighting the Axis, not the leftists among their allies.

FIFTEEN

Orazio and Sebastian bent over the papers that littered the table in the breakfast room.

'Please tell me this is the last one,' Sebastian said, scribbling his name at the bottom of an impressive document with a silk tassel dangling from it.

'It is,' Orazio said.

'At last.'

'And here is the copy of your new will, sent over by the attorney's office.'

'What a relief,' Sebastian said. 'I am so glad it's finished. What if I should die before Alessa and we have no children yet? What if we don't have any children at all? I want to make sure she inherits what money I am able to leave her. I can't prevent my cousin from inheriting the title or the entailed property, but I can make sure that Alessa receives the remainder.'

'Your mother won't like the idea of breaking up the estate,' Orazio said.

'That's why I'm not telling her,' Sebastian said. Both men laughed. 'Besides, it's only a precaution. Alessa and I plan to have many

122

children as soon as possible. Mamma will immediately adore them, and all will be well between her and my wife.'

Sebastian slid the will into a plain brown envelope and sealed it. 'I know the attorney has a copy of the new will, but this one ought to go into my safety deposit box in the bank in New York. I don't want it in the apartment. It would be so unpleasant if my mother should find it.'

'These papers should go to the bank, too,' Orazio said, patting the impressive stack, thick with seals and more tassels, on the table between them. 'All the deeds and such that the lawyer needed to draw up your will.'

'It's absurd to travel all the way to New York to store these documents,' Sebastian said. 'But there's not an available safety deposit box in all of Washington, DC! And did you know the hotel safe is full, too? Not to mention that it's opened dozens of time a day so women can access their jewelry.'

'I have an idea,' Orazio said.

The two men paused while Lina came into the breakfast room and removed their tea-cups.

'I could ride up to New York on the train with Alessa,' Orazio said. 'I'll stay with my cousin on Staten Island. In the meantime I'll deposit these papers in the bank, and your mother will never know I went on business. Then I'll return on the train with Alessa.'

Sebastian clapped a hand on his shoulder. *'Brilliante,'* he said. 'You deserve a holiday. This way Mamma will have no idea you're on a business trip, and Alessa will have a chaperone on the train.'

I waited in one of the longest lines I think I'd ever seen for a bus, and that was saying something. It was raining, a heavy pounding rain that obscured windshields and made changing lanes treacherous, so cars weren't stopping to pick up people from the slug lines as usual. I shared my umbrella with a shivering young woman from Codes and Cables. At the rate the buses came by, I figured it would be two hours before I got home.

A green Lincoln Continental cabriolet pulled up next to me, and Joan leaned over to roll down the window. 'Climb in,' she said. 'Let's go to my place.'

'That depends,' I answered. 'Are you going to shine a bright spotlight on my face and interrogate me?'

'Absolutely not. Your examination is over, and you passed with flying colors. I'm going to make you a Martini, and we're going to order room service!'

'If you think you can bribe me to forgive you, you're so right!' I lent my umbrella to the Codes and Cables girl and climbed into the passenger seat of Joan's grand car. We pulled away from the curb and headed east.

Joan was a wealthy young woman. She owned a car and received a hundred dollar a month allowance from her parents in addition to her OSS salary. She'd graduated from Smith College and was one of Director Donovan's two trusted secretaries. Joan had countless friends but no beau, which was what she wanted more than anything else in the world. Maybe it was her height or her booming voice or her large personality that prevented her from attracting men.

Joan was one of the few single people I knew who had her own place, a fancy hotel studio apartment that I coveted with all my heart and soul. She dropped me off at the residents' entrance on De Sales Street while she parked her car. I passed the time chatting with Hays, the concierge, until she joined me and we went upstairs.

Once inside Joan's apartment I transformed her rumpled Pullman davenport bed back into a sofa while she went into her kitchenette to fix our drinks.

'There's a room service menu on the table near the door,' she called out. 'It's a new one. What looks good? We should order now; sometimes dinner takes an hour to arrive.'

I intended to pay for my own meal, so the beef entrée, Swiss steak, was out of the question.

'Fried chicken?' I called out. 'Chicken à la

King? Chicken Marengo?'

'Order me the fried chicken,' she answered from the kitchenette. Dellaphine fixed her scrumptious fried chicken once a week, so I settled on chicken à la king. I made sure that room service knew I needed a chit to pay for my order.

After I hung up I called 'Two Trees' and told Phoebe I wouldn't be home for dinner that night.

Joan brought out a silver cocktail tray holding a shaker, two Martini glasses and a bowl of nuts. 'No olive, correct?' she asked.

'Please,' I said. 'I haven't developed a taste for olives. Or caviar.'

We sipped from our glasses.

'That's so good,' I said. 'Do you know I never had a cocktail until I moved to Washington?'

'What do your people in North Carolina think of you now?'

'I haven't been back home. And I haven't written them much about what's happened to me. I'm afraid it would shock them terribly. Both sets of my grandparents are spinning wildly in their graves as we speak.'

'So,' Joan said, crossing her legs, 'what have you developed a taste for, if not olives and caviar?'

'Let's see. Cocktails, definitely. A paycheck, no question. Shopping with my own money. Having lots of friends, all kinds. Feeling

126

useful and good at my job.' Not living with my parents. Not working for my parents. Not going to church. Not having the neighbors comment on whether I'm going to church. Not being forced to consider every breathing single man I met as a potential second husband in order to escape my parents' house. The list was very, very long.

'Another Martini?' she asked.

'Better not,' I answered. 'Work tomorrow.'

We played gin rummy and listened to the radio until dinner came. The food was good, but eating it off dishes stamped with the famous ship in full sail would have been fun even if the food was terrible.

SIXTEEN

If Lucia Oneto hadn't had her back to the window of the Presidential Restaurant, and if Louise hadn't been hurrying down De Sales Street under an umbrella borrowed from Joan to find a taxi, Louise might have recognized the Dowager Countess. But she'd never met Sebastian, who faced the window, and she was too intent on getting out of the cold rain to care who was dining at the premier restaurant of the Mayflower Hotel.

'This is lovely,' Lucia said, daintily using her oyster fork to scoop up her scalloped oysters, 'to be able to dine with you alone. Not that I'm not fond of Alessa, you understand, but once a son is married, a mother doesn't have him to herself much. And Orazio absent at the same time! I realize he is a great help to you, but to live in such close quarters!'

'I understand, Mamma,' Sebastian said, determined to humor his mother tonight. She could be unbearably irritating at times, but she was miles away from her home, friends, and her usual pleasures, and he tried to take that into account. He'd ordered a bottle of expensive wine for them to split, and by God, it did taste wonderful. And steaks, an extravagance, but he wanted this meal to be a treat for his mother. What did she have to do here? She couldn't go to the market, have her parties, meet her friends for cards and tea, or give out prizes at the village school.

Sebastian usually avoided the hotel restaurants, preferring room service. Most of the men who dined in the hotel restaurants wore uniforms, and it grated on him that he couldn't serve in the military. And he possessed no skills that were useful in any of the wartime bureaucracies. In times like these, who needed a student of nineteenth century Italian literature and citrus horticulture? He knew most Americans resented wealthy Europeans living in their midst while American boys risked their lives to save the foreigners' homelands. All he could do was squeeze as much money out of his income as possible to give to wartime charities.

Sebastian poured them each another glass of wine from the bottle that sat in a silver bucket next to his right hand.

'I didn't know Orazio had a cousin in New York,' Lucia said, after sipping her wine.

'Most Italians have relatives in the United States now, Mamma, thanks to Mussolini forcing so many into exile.'

Lucia toyed with her wine glass and watched the rich red liquid swirl around its sides while Sebastian finished his prawns. 'Does Alessa have a relative in New York City, dear?' she asked.

Sebastian wiped his mouth and signaled for the waiter to take away their appetizer plates. The pause failed to help him keep his temper. 'For God's sake, Mamma!'

'Well, does she? And is she visiting him?'

'Yes, Turi lives in New York City. I understand he works on the docks. I hope Alessa does visit him.'

Lucia drained her glass. 'How can you say such a thing! His origins! How did he get here?'

'So Alessa's father had an affair with a pretty peasant girl as a teenager. It happens. He did the right thing and took care of the boy.'

'She wasn't just a peasant girl,' Lucia said. She lowered her voice. 'Her family was *Mafioso*! So degrading!'

'I'm going to say this once, Mamma, and you will never mention it again. Alessa's father helped Turi escape to America years ago, when Mussolini destroyed the *Mafioso* and most of them fled Sicily. He is an honest workingman now and Alessa's only blood relative. She is welcome to see him.'

'Your father would be ashamed.'

'Father is dead, along with his time. Now

enjoy your steak and we will talk of something else, like our tickets to the USO benefit ball next week. What gown do you plan to wear?'

SEVENTEEN

It was late when my taxi dropped me off at the door of 'Two Trees'. The rain had stopped, but icy, fat raindrops fell from the trees with every cold breeze. I'd expected the house to be dark, but the downstairs lights were still on, and once inside I heard both radios – one in the lounge, and one in the kitchen – blaring, with the voices of my fellow residents chattering over the sound of the news. When I entered the lounge I found Phoebe, Joe, and Henry. Ada was at work. The news ended as I came in, followed by the theme music for the Red Skelton Show. Joe turned the volume down.

Phoebe gathered her skirts and slid over to make room for me on the davenport.

'What's going on?' I asked.

'President Roosevelt just finished speaking,' Phoebe said.

'Good news,' Henry said, 'and lots of it! We have won Guadalcanal! The Japanese Armada has been smashed! The Japs lost twenty-three ships and twenty-five thousand men! Admiral Halsey's a hero!'

'It was bloody close,' Joe said, with his usual calm pragmatism. 'Too close. If the Japs destroyed Henderson Air Field and our bombers, we wouldn't have had a chance.'

Joe turned to me with a significant look. 'The Vichy French forces in North Africa have turned on the Nazis,' he said. 'They're fighting right alongside the Allies.' Rachel's husband Gerald was supposed to be part of the French Resistance there, if he was still alive.

'The French!' Henry snorted. 'Never know what side they're on.'

'Ever experienced a Nazi occupation, Henry?' Joe asked quietly. 'Sometimes not resisting is the wisest choice, especially when your family's lives are at stake.'

'Do you have to work on Thanksgiving Day, Louise?' Phoebe asked, quickly changing the subject.

I hadn't given Thanksgiving any thought at all. 'I would expect so,' I said.

'When is Thanksgiving?' Joe asked.

'Thursday next week.'

'A weekday. I'll be working, I'm sure.'

'I guess we'll be skipping Thanksgiving this year,' Henry said. 'We'll make do with a prayer for the troops.'

'Nonsense,' Phoebe said. 'As long as I am alive we will have Thanksgiving dinner in this house. Dellaphine and I will cook during the day, and we'll eat during our usual dinner hour. Turkey and all the usual side dishes, with sherry before.'

'But Phoebe,' I said, 'turkey is forty-two cents a pound! I saw it in the Safeway ad.'

'I can manage it, if you all are willing to eat macaroni and cheese and scalloped potatoes and bacon for dinner early in the week.'

We were willing.

I went back to the kitchen for a glass of water and found Madeleine seated at the table with her elbows on the table and her head in her hands. Her eyes were swollen from crying. She was dressed for bed in flannel pajamas and a fuzzy bathrobe.

'Are you OK?' I asked.

'I'm so disappointed,' Madeleine said. 'Three of my girlfriends and I've been looking for an apartment to share. We can afford it. We all live with our folks, and we want to get out on our own.'

'Sounds like fun,' I said.

'For the last month we've looked everywhere. No one will rent an apartment to colored girls. No one. Nowhere. No matter how much deposit money we got or how good our references are. We're all government girls, too.'

'Dearie, I am so sorry. I know it must be tough to share a room with your mother.' I couldn't imagine it.

'It's tiresome,' she said. 'And crowded. She knows what I'm doing every minute. I can't have friends over.'

'What about the colored girls who've come to Washington from out of town?'

'There are colored boarding-houses, and the government has built barracks for them.'

'I don't know what to say. I wish it weren't so.'

Madeleine dropped her head back into her hands, then lifted it again, forcing a look of resolution on to her face. 'I guess I can save more money this way. I'd like to go to Howard after the war.'

'I'm going to college too, I hope,' I said. 'And I can't afford an apartment either.'

'Big difference between you and me is, somebody would rent to you.'

As I walked down the hall back to the lounge I said a prayer that colored people like Madeleine would be better off after the war, after they'd proved they could fight and work as well as anyone else. As long as there were people like Henry in the world it would be a struggle.

I went into the lounge saying yet another prayer, that Joe would be alone there. He wasn't. Henry still sat in his usual chair reading a newspaper. Why in God's name couldn't he read in his room?

Phoebe checked into the lounge on her way upstairs. 'It's late,' she said. 'Coming to bed, Louise? I'll walk upstairs with you.'

'Sure,' I said.

Joe shot me a look of resignation and regret that made my knees wobble.

EIGHTEEN

Tuesday morning. Four days until I met with Alessa again.

I sat at my desk behind my partition, the closest to private space I had, but it was difficult to work. Friday seemed like an eternity from now.

And Betty was still absent! Sure, I was worried about her health, but I worried as much about work. Betty was young and silly, but she was a terrific typist and I didn't want to have to replace her. I wondered again if something more dire than illness was going on in her life.

'Ruth, Brenda, can you manage without me for a while?' I asked. 'I'm going to take a long lunch hour and go over to Betty's boarding house and see how she is.'

'We'll be fine,' Brenda said. 'Things are quiet right now.'

'I'm glad you're going to check on her,' Ruth said. 'I've been worried.'

Betty's boarding house couldn't have been more different from 'Two Trees' if it was on the moon. It was five stories tall, halfway down a long street of identical town houses, each one as shabby as the rest.

The brick facade was painted a deep green, now faded to a flat pea green in patches where the sun lingered. Shades hung to the sills in all the windows, making the house look as though it was napping. The tiny front yard, though swept and weedless, was bare of anything green.

When I knocked at the door a middle-aged white woman opened it with a do-rag wrapped around her head, carrying an armload of frayed sheets.

'And you are?' she asked.

'I'm Louise Pearlie,' I said. 'Betty works for me. She hasn't come to the office in several days, and I understand she's ill? I'm worried about her. Could I see her, please?'

'She ain't here,' the woman said.

'What do you mean?'

'I mean she ain't here. For almost a week now. Her rent's paid up through the month, though, so I expect she'll be back. Her room-mates said she got a week's vacation. I didn't know government girls got that kind of time off.'

I must have looked awfully surprised, because the woman sighed in resignation, and ushered me into the dark hall.

'You'd better come in,' she said. 'I'm Eloise Brown. I own this place.'

The hall was dark and needed new wallpaper, but was otherwise clean. A steep, narrow set of stairs led up into darkness.

'One of Betty's room-mates works second shift; I'm pretty sure she's in,' Mrs Brown said. 'Why don't you go on up and talk to her? Room Three-Oh-Three.'

I flicked on the light switch before starting up the steep narrow stairs. Nothing happened, and I noticed the ceiling light socket was empty.

Seeing my hesitation, the landlady said, 'We don't waste power here, like the President says.'

I don't think the President wants me to fall down the stairs and break my neck, I thought as I felt my way to the top of the staircase, caught my breath on the landing, and headed up another steep flight.

There were three rooms on the third floor. I glanced into the single bathroom and saw an outdated bathroom suite and worn linoleum, although it seemed clean enough.

I knocked on the door of Room 303, and a girl called out to me.

'Come on the hell in!' Her voice sounded familiar.

I opened the door and found that I needed to edge my way inside. Three twin beds and one tall dresser filled the space, with barely enough room to move between them. Drying laundry hung from the curtain rods, and

139

suitcases poked out from under the beds. There was nowhere to sit other than on the beds themselves.

And on the bed farthest from me, under the only window, propped up on pillows, sat Myrna, painting her fingernails scarlet.

'Well, I'll be damned,' she said. 'Louise! What are you doing here?'

'Betty works for me,' I said, so amazed to see her that I stopped dead inside the doorway and stared.

'Oh, Lord,' Myrna said, 'you're that Louise! Betty talks about you all the time. Small world. Come on in.'

Myrna slung her pajama-clad legs off the edge of her bed and let them dangle off the side.

'Come on over here and sit,' she said, patting the bed next to hers.

I threaded my way through the room and sat. I was terribly curious, but knew better than to ask Myrna anything about her job, her work, or our time at 'The Farm' together.

'What on earth is going on?' I asked. 'Betty called in sick days ago, and now her landlady says she's on a holiday? This is serious. She could lose her job.'

Myrna didn't answer for a minute. 'It's already serious.'

The worse possibility I could think of crossed my mind. 'An abortion?' I asked.

140

'No, thank goodness,' Myrna said. 'But it's bad. Lil, our other room-mate, and I've been covering for her every way we know how, hoping she'd get back soon and go back to work without anyone knowing.'

'Knowing what?'

'She's in jail.'

NINETEEN

'Excuse me?' I said. 'I thought I heard you say Betty was in jail?'

'She was arrested Tuesday, so early in the morning that no one had left for work yet. The police came and handcuffed her. She screamed and cried and begged. Lil and I screamed and argued. All the other girls gathered in the hall downstairs and watched the police drag her away. They stuck her in the back of a paddy wagon with a bunch of prostitutes. She's in a real jam.'

A dozen images came to my mind, among them Betty shoplifting or dealing in the black market, but I discarded them all. The girl wasn't a criminal.

'What was she charged with? It must be a mistake!'

'No mistake,' Myrna said, lighting a cigarette and holding it gingerly away from her drying fingernails. 'She was arrested because she could have venereal disease.'

Of course I was shocked. How devastating for her! All that boy-craziness had finally caught up with Betty, but I still didn't under-

142

stand why she was in jail.

'You can get arrested for having VD?' I asked.

'Only if you're a woman,' Myrna said. 'What happens is, when some soldier or sailor gets clap, he has to tell the pecker-checker about all the good-time girls he's been with over the past six months if he wants to avoid the brig. Some squid Betty dumped months ago turned her in. So she gets carted off to jail until her blood test comes back.'

'Why on earth?' I asked.

'To keep her from infecting some other innocent farm boy.'

'Some boy infected her first!'

'Of course, but men have to be free to fight the war.'

'So what happens next?'

'If her test is negative she goes free. If not, she's sent to a quarantine hospital for treatment. It's prison, actually.'

'What happens to the sailor?'

'Oh, he sits around sick bay in his pajamas and takes sulfa pills until he's cured, and then he goes back on duty.'

'While the woman he's named is ruined.'

'Yeah. Ain't life swell?'

The injustice of Betty's predicament enraged me. I'd been raised to keep most of my thoughts to myself, but in this case I couldn't keep quiet. Oh, I'd heard all about Eliot

Ness and his Committee on Social Protection. Promiscuous women were responsible for the spread of VD in the armed forces. Men had needs they couldn't be expected to control; besides, they had to fight. Fighting men were important, women were expendable.

'Sanctimonious bastards,' I said. 'If Betty has clap it's because some fast-talking man gave it to her first!'

'Louise, your vehemence surprises me. It's not like you.'

'Where is Betty? Have you been to see her? When will her test be returned?'

'In the DC jail, no, and I think any day now. What are you going to do?'

'I don't know.' And I didn't.

'Let me know if I can help.'

I left Myrna separating her toes with cotton so she could paint them to match her fingernails.

I was too upset and angry to go straight back to work, so I went down the street until I found a café and ducked inside.

'You don't by some chance have any coffee, do you?' I asked. I felt cold, and it wasn't the weather.

'In fact, we do,' the waitress said. 'I think there's half a pot left. Want a cup?'

'Please,' I said. 'Anything sweet? At all? I don't care what it is.'

'I think there's some apple pie, but it's made with honey.'

'I'll have a slice.'

The waitress brought my order right away. She was young, maybe fifteen, with a long ponytail and too much make-up. I badly wanted to warn her to stay away from GIs frantic for sex before they got shipped off to some battlefield, but I didn't. It wouldn't do any good, anyway.

Ever since the war started, young men and women were thrown together far away from hometowns, families, and churches. They had money in their pockets and the freedom to do as they wished. Having sex without marriage became part of the adventure. I mean, wasn't I thinking of having an affair myself, something I would never have dreamed of even one short year ago? Joe and I weren't willing to resort to the back seat of Phoebe's car or some cold park bench, but plenty were.

Good-time girls, pick-ups, victory girls, whatever you wanted to call them, were just one tryst away from disease, pregnancy, or a ruined 'reputation' that would follow them the rest of their lives. The men? They were heroes who couldn't be expected to turn down a fling before going to war, egged on by suggestive pin-ups, barbershop magazines, and movies. At the same time women, from USO hostesses to factory workers, were admonished to dress up and be 'nice' to our fighting men.

Coffee, apple pie, and time calmed me down. I couldn't do a damn thing about most of this, but maybe I could help Betty survive. If she wasn't infected, that was.

TWENTY

It was almost dusk, but Alessa felt quite safe, even if she was sitting smack dab in the middle of Central Park on a bench under a cluster of evergreen trees. It was a mild day for New York City in November. The park was full of servicemen walking with their sweeties and nursemaids pushing carriages. Men and women strolled home in pairs with their tennis rackets or croquet mallets over their shoulders. Besides, the Swedish Cottage, with its charming peaked roof and arched windows, was just around the pathway bend. It housed the Civil Defense headquarters of New York City. If she screamed, which she certainly would have no need to, dozens of men with batons and helmets would rush to her defense.

Turi slid on to the bench beside her. '*Cara mia*,' he said, embracing her.

'It makes me so happy to see you,' Alessa said, holding on to him tightly.

The two untangled themselves, and Turi lit a cigarette.

'So,' he said, 'how is it going?'

147

'Fine,' Alessa said. 'Louise has no idea who I am. After I hand over the name you give me, she'll take it to her handler – that's a spy word.'

'I know,' Turi said, smiling at her.

'Then it's over.' She took his arm. 'Turi,' she asked, 'please can I keep going to the knitting circle? I would stay in my disguise. Louise is the first real friend I've made here.'

Her brother shook his head and squeezed her hand. 'It's far too dangerous,' he said. 'When you told me you lived in Washington, well, I saw the chance to get this information to the authorities without getting me and my family killed. I don't want anything to happen to you either.'

'If you insist,' she said, patting his hand. 'It's worth it to be able to do something important. I felt so useless sitting around the apartment waiting for the war to end.'

'Here,' he said, handing her an envelope and a folded sheet of paper. She took it, but he wrapped both of his hands around hers.

'Dear one,' he said, 'you must never, ever, say this name aloud. For the rest of your life.' He released her hand, and she read the name on the paper. Blood drained from her face.

'Oh, Turi, I've seen his name in the newspaper,' she whispered.

'Oh, many times, I'm sure.' Turi grimaced. 'He's a powerful man.'

'I don't understand. Turi, he's Mafia.'

'He's a *capobastone*, an underboss, and I am one of his *capodecina*.'

'No! You promised father!' Alessa pulled her hand from his arm and struck him. 'You're not! Why!'

Without speaking, Turi pulled a thick rolled up wad of bills from his pocket and showed it to her, then stuffed it back into his shirt.

'How could you risk your life so!'

'Pfft. It's not dangerous. Unless you overhear your *capobastone* talking to a German in a restaurant bathroom. They spoke Italian, but the stranger had a strong German accent, so I raised my feet above the floor and kept silent. They thought they were alone. What they said froze my blood. I learned that my *capobastone* is a traitor. He is giving the Germans information about our convoys.'

'Oh, Turi!'

'You see, the Mafia run the docks and the unions,' he said. '"Socks" Lanza, he made a deal with the Office of Naval Intelligence to keep the East Side safe for American shipping. Then "Lucky" Luciano, he does the same for the West Side. Dock workers, stevedores, stewards, and fishermen, we're proud to be patriots and spies for the US of A. Except for the sleepers Mussolini and the Nazis planted before the war even began.'

'I thought Luciano was in jail.'

'Yeah, and he doesn't like it much, even though he has his own personal chef. He wants parole. Meyer Lansky is running his operation for him while he's inside. Christ, Lansky hates the Nazis. He's a Yid, you know. Sometimes I think there're more Yids in the mob than Italians!

'Your *capobastone*, why does he do this?'

Turi shrugged. 'I don't know,' he said. 'And if he suspected I knew his plans...' Turi drew an invisible knife across his throat.

'Don't do that!' Alessa said.

'Now because of you I don't have to watch this awful man feed information to the Nazis.'

'But if,' Alessa said as she looked around to see if anyone was nearby, 'the man is guilty, why would anyone hurt you?'

'Wouldn't matter. You know of *omertà*, the code of silence? If I break it, I am a rat. Rats die. So,' he said, 'you give that name to your friend Louise and forget you ever saw it.'

'When am I going to see you again? Meet your wife and children?'

'Soon,' he said. 'After all this is ended.'

TWENTY-ONE

The District of Columbia jail was ugly when it was built in 1895. Now that its facade was coated with years of grime and soot it looked like an abandoned factory, except for the police cars and paddy wagons lined up outside. Even here you could tell there was a war on. A couple of Army jeeps manned by military policemen parked among the police cars. I supposed they were there to pick up soldiers who'd gotten arrested the night before.

I attracted plenty of notice as I walked up the broad cement steps and into the lobby. I was the only woman in sight. Resolutely, I ignored the stares of the policemen and the crowd of crime reporters and photographers who sprawled on benches around the lobby. I presented myself at the reception desk, a heavy wooden counter topped with bars that reached to the ceiling.

'Yes, ma'am?' the sergeant on duty asked.

'I want to visit a prisoner,' I said. 'She works for me, and I just learned today that she's here.'

'I'm sorry, but it ain't visiting hours,' he said.

I focused on keeping my voice calm and steady. 'I understand that she was arrested for possibly having venereal disease.'

'Oh,' the sergeant said, wrinkling his nose as though he'd gotten a whiff of a bad odor. 'One of them girls. They ain't exactly arrested, just taken into custody.'

What was the difference, I wondered?

'They're in a special ward. You can go on back there. Mike,' he called out to a policeman walking through the lobby, 'take—' and he looked at me questioningly.

'Mrs Louise Pearlie,' I said.

'Take Mrs Pearlie back to the women's quarantined ward,' he said.

Mike was white-haired and stooped. I guessed he'd be retired if it weren't for the war. He led me through a vast hall four stories tall, stacked with barred cells from floor to ceiling, all reached by what looked like fire escapes. There was a large blackboard in the middle of the hall surrounded by metal chairs.

'That's where the illiterate prisoners are supposed to learn to read,' Mike said. 'Most of them don't do too good. But Mrs Roosevelt is big on rehabilitation, so we got to try to teach them something.'

Through a door at the far end of the vast space we found ourselves in a one-story

152

corridor that led to a wall of bars with another door set into it. Mike rang a bell, and another guard appeared.

'Mrs Pearlie here wants to see one of the sluts,' he said. If Mike was expecting a rise from me, he didn't get it. It wouldn't help Betty if I made a scene. If I was to help her slip back into a normal life, the less memorable we both were the better.

Officer Runyan, according to his name tag, led me past a couple of cells. There were no female guards that I could see. We reached one occupied by four women lying on the bare mattresses of two bunk beds. There was nowhere else to sit.

The guard put a key in the lock and opened the door with a clang. 'Betty, girl, you got a visitor,' he called out. 'Fifteen minutes,' he said to me.

Betty instantly sat up from where she was curled up on a lower bunk. Two other women, wrapped in blankets, rolled over on their bunks to get a look at me, then rolled back to go back to sleep.

I sat down next to Betty, and she burst into hysterical sobs. I took her in my arms. She hadn't bathed in days. Her hair was filthy and stringy, and dirt showed beneath her fingernails.

'How did you find out?' she said, between sobs.

'I went to your boarding house, and Myrna

told me,' I said.

'I want to kill myself,' she said, 'I really do. I'm ruined!'

I took her by both arms and shook her. 'Don't be stupid,' I said. 'You're only ruined if you allow it to happen.'

'That sailor lied! I didn't sleep with him! He was getting back at me for dumping him!'

I resisted the urge to take her by the shoulders and shake her again, this time until her teeth rattled. 'I don't care if you've screwed a dozen men,' I said. 'If that test comes back negative, you pull yourself together and come back to work. You can bet that's what he's doing; he's not giving you, or the fact that he had clap, a second thought. He's going on with his life.'

'You won't tell?'

'Why would I do that? You've been ill. After you recover you'll return to work.' I took her face in my hands. 'Tell me the truth,' I said. 'Do you think you've got it?'

'No,' she said. 'I don't have any of the symptoms.' She burst into tears again. 'No one will ever marry me now.'

'Shut up,' I said, 'and listen to me. When you get your test back tomorrow, if it's negative, what happens?'

'They release me, and I go jump off the Washington Monument.'

'Be serious.'

'They release me, and then I don't know.'

'Do you have any money?'

She shook her head.

'Here,' I said, digging into my handbag. 'Here's five dollars. Get a taxi and go back to your boarding house.'

'I can't. I can't face my friends. You don't know what it was like! They put me in a paddy wagon with prostitutes and drunks!'

'Stop it, or I'll walk out of here right now. I mean it! Here,' I said, giving her my clean handkerchief.

Slowly, Betty stopped sniffling.

'You go back to your boarding house tomorrow,' I said. 'You tell everyone that you have been horribly wronged. This soldier—'

'Sailor,' she interrupted.

'This sailor you dated, he turned you in to get back at you for not putting out, get it? You stick to that story, understand? And cry a lot. No one can prove it's not true.'

'OK,' she said. 'Gary, that's his name, had to give girls' names to the pecker-checker, or he would have been sent to the brig. So he got back at me!'

'That's it. He'll be shipped out soon, if he hasn't been already.'

'With luck he'll get shot in his dick. That's what he deserves,' one of the other women said, without turning around to face us.

'When you get home clean yourself up,' I said to Betty. 'You'll feel better. Myrna and

Lil will help you. Myrna has the number of my boarding house, and she'll call me to let me know you're home. Then the next day, you come to work, maybe still feeling a little poorly.'

She cringed. 'I don't know if I can,' she said.

'If you don't show up by nine thirty, I'm coming for you in a taxi, and I'll drag you back to the office by your hair. Got it?'

'Do you think it will work?'

'Of course it will work. Your girlfriends won't let you down. And any possible record you might have is buried deep in a file cabinet in a basement somewhere. After the war they'll make bonfires of all that paper.'

Betty wiped her eyes with the dingy sleeves of her striped prison housecoat. 'Thank you,' she said.

'Forget it.'

Betty'd been a little fool, but she was a damn good typist, and I didn't want to even think about how difficult it would be to replace her.

TWENTY-TWO

'How's Betty?' Brenda asked.

I needed to be careful about what I answered. I couldn't lie to anyone at OSS, but I wanted to give Betty a chance to return.

'Not well,' I said. 'But I hope she'll be back soon.'

'Don wants you in his office,' Ruth said. 'You sure you two aren't an item again?'

'Never! Don't even let that cross your mind! It's that special job I did for him, sorting the postcards, you know? Apparently, I'm now the go-to girl for all his projects.'

Melinsky waited for me alone in Don's office. He wore his tailored uniform today. With his legs crossed, puffing on one of his imported cigarettes, he could have been sitting in the morning room of an estate, waiting for his steward to brief him on the progress of the spring lambing.

Melinsky stubbed out his cigarette and gestured for me to sit down. 'We need to discuss tomorrow night,' he said. 'There's no reason to think anything untoward will happen, but we must make plans for every eventuality.'

'All right,' I said. My pulse quickened.

'First, what we know about the Oneto family.' Melinsky proceeded to brief me on the contents of the Oneto OSS file, which I'd already read, while I nodded as if it was news to me.

'Of course, we have done some additional research,' Melinsky said. 'We've found that here in Washington the Onetos live at the Mayflower hotel.'

'Really?' I said. My friend Joan's studio apartment was in the Mayflower.

'The Onetos rent a big apartment there,' Melinsky said. 'The household includes Count Sebastian; his wife, Alessa; his mother, Lucia; a maid; and a private secretary. All with unsurprising backgrounds. Typical exiles waiting out the war in safety, although the Count has tried to enlist, I'll give him that. Flunked all his physicals. Terrible vision and a heart murmur.'

I wondered what sort of man Alessa was married to. She was a good, brave woman, and I hoped the Count was worthy of her.

Two Army privates wrapped in greatcoats, their breath steaming, passed by the window with their guns at the ready. They were part of the detail that protected our grounds, and they couldn't have overheard us, anyway, but

Melinsky waited for their footsteps to fade away before he spoke again.

'Alessa and the private secretary, a man named Rossi, took the train to New York on Tuesday,' he said.

'I thought you weren't going to follow her!'

'I felt it was necessary, but he went no further than the Union Station. Another of our men picked up the tail in New York. Alessa caught a taxi and took it to a residential hotel. Rossi boarded the Staten Island Ferry. No one else followed either of them. Our man verified that their return tickets were for today. So Alessa will be back in town for your knitting circle tomorrow night.'

'Do you think she retrieved the "take" from her asset in New York?'

'I don't want to speculate, but it seems very likely.' Melinsky uncrossed his legs and pulled his chair up to the desk, leaning forward. 'Tomorrow night you will have a babysitter, just in case,' he said.

My mouth went dry, and my already rapid heartbeat began to race.

'You'll have a new addition to your knitting group. She is an experienced agent and will be armed. She's a good knitter, too, I understand!' He smiled, but when I didn't seem amused, he continued. 'Whether or not you receive anything from Alessa, you'll leave with our agent, you know, chatting, two women getting to know each other and such. Instead of going to the filling station, the two of you will walk further down Twenty-First to the Western Market, which is open late on Friday night.'

And right next door to a police station, I thought. Just in case.

'Our agent, whose cover name is Anne, by the way, will escort you out the back door of the market. Jack will be waiting there with a car to bring you to me. With what we expect, I hope. The name of our sleeper.'

I was hanging up my coat when Ada answered the telephone in the hall.

'She just got home,' Ada said into the receiver. 'Here she is.' She handed the telephone to me. It was Myrna.

'Betty's test was negative, and she's here safe and sound,' Myrna said. 'Soaking in the bath. What did you say to her? She seems quite calm.'

'I talked some sense into her,' I said. 'It's up to you and Lil to make it stick. She has to come to work tomorrow and behave as if she's returned from an illness. If she can keep herself together she can beat this.'

'I'll tie her up and deliver her myself if I have to,' Myrna said.

'OK. Tell her I haven't said a word to anyone, even Ruth and Brenda. No one ever needs to know.'

160

'I've told everyone here she was wronged by an old beau. All the girls sympathize with that. Hey, I've got someone waiting for the phone, so I have to ring off.'

'Thanks.'

'Not necessary.'

I replaced the receiver. I'd done all I could for Betty. Now it was up to her to behave like an adult woman, not a prisoner of her raising and the women's magazines she pored over, and live her life the way she wanted to live it.

I was beat from my dealings with Betty and Melinsky and nervous about meeting Alessa, maybe for the last time, tomorrow evening. I needed a good dinner, maybe an hour of radio – no news, thank you – and one of Phoebe's Nembutals so I could sleep to-night. I wished I could have one Martini! Tomorrow promised to be a nerve-wracking day.

As I went back to the kitchen for a glass of water I met Ada coming down the hall.

'I wouldn't go in there if I was you,' she said and vanished into the lounge.

I soon wished I'd listened to her.

Dellaphine's big Silvertone radio played gospel music softly as she finished arranging yeast rolls in a baking pan. The odor of roast chicken seasoned with onions and sage filled the room. Madeleine had arrived home from work. She was still dressed in office clothes,

161

a neat green shirtwaist dress with a lace collar.

Phoebe stood next to the table, her arms crossed, while Joe was trapped between the Hoosier cabinet and Phoebe, with no way to leave the kitchen, though he sure looked like he wanted to.

Henry, who was clearly the source of whatever trouble was brewing, stood at the table with his laundry bag slumped on one of the kitchen chairs.

'I don't understand the problem,' Henry said. 'I've been to three laundries today, and not one of them is accepting any new customers! Have you ever heard of such a thing! One of those damn Chinks suggested I send my laundry home!'

'Dellaphine doesn't do any personal laundry,' Phoebe said. 'She has more than enough work to do: most of the cooking and cleaning, laundering the sheets and towels, queuing for groceries.' Phoebe spoke firmly. She was clear-eyed, so she must not have dosed herself with laudanum today.

'But I'd pay her extra!'

'She's not your laundress,' Phoebe said. 'You're responsible for your own laundry.'

Dellaphine didn't say a word, but kept neatly lining up doughy rolls in the baking pan.

Then, so help me, Henry looked right at Madeleine, and I waited for, I didn't know what, some awful eruption. But Madeleine controlled her temper. She looked straight into Henry's eyes.

'I have a job, Mr Post,' she said. 'And it doesn't include taking in laundry.'

'So what am I supposed to do?' Henry said, staring helplessly at his laundry bag.

The kitchen timer dinged, and Phoebe went over to the stove, opening a path for Joe's escape, which he took with alacrity.

'The rest of us do our own laundry,' I said to Henry. 'There's a perfectly good new Bendix washing machine in the basement and plenty of drying lines.'

'But you're women,' Henry said.

'Henry,' I said, 'I'll tell you what. Over the weekend I'll teach you to use the washing machine. One lesson should do it.'

'What are we coming to,' Henry said, 'when a man has to do his own laundry! And what about ironing?'

Dellaphine stood, the pan of rolls in her hand to set in the oven. 'I been ironing since I was nine years old,' she said. 'I'll show you how to iron. Once.'

'You all get out of this kitchen,' Phoebe said, 'and let Dellaphine and me get dinner on the table.'

Henry and I joined Ada and Joe in the lounge.

To signal that disaster was averted, I said, 'I'm going to show Henry how to use the washing machine, and Dellaphine is going to teach him how to iron.'

I should have known to keep my mouth shut. A hot red flush crawled up Henry's neck and face, and we saw the ugliness of the anger he'd hidden in the kitchen.

'These people, these Chink laundrymen, the Negroes, they'll be begging to do our laundry again after the war, you wait and see!'

'Shut up, Henry,' Ada said as Joe turned up the volume on the radio to drown him out.

Joe and I spent a few minutes alone together in the lounge after dinner. Or what passed for alone in that house. Phoebe and Ada were in the kitchen, making tea I assumed, because I heard the rattle of cups and saucers.

Joe joined me on the sofa and I curled up in his arms.

'So,' I said, 'who washes your clothes? Somehow you escaped telling us.'

Joe groaned. 'One of my friends at work, his mother takes in laundry. I take my laundry to the office and pick it up two days later.'

'Perhaps Henry could avoid the humiliation of women's work if your woman would do his, too.'

'I am not carrying Henry's laundry bag anywhere. He deserves this lesson. Can we

164

forget about washing and such for the few minutes we've been left in blessed solitude?'

We kissed, the longest kiss we'd been able to share in many days. His soft beard nuzzled my face while he caressed my bottom with one hand, the one that wasn't holding me close. I didn't feel the usual tingle, though, I suppose because I was preoccupied with my Friday evening meeting with Alessa.

'Are you OK?' Joe asked. 'You're trembling.' He pulled Phoebe's embroidered throw over my shoulders.

'I'm tired,' I said. 'Work has been difficult, with this special project and with making sure the usual office stuff gets done, and one of my girls is out sick.'

'Let's go out somewhere tomorrow night,' he said. 'Get a drink and have dinner. We'll stay out of public parks.'

'I'd love to,' I said, 'but I have to go to my knitting circle.'

'Can't you skip it once?'

'I can't.' I tried to think of a good reason. 'I'm supposed to get a coffee afterwards with one of the women.'

'Saturday night, then?'

'Yes, that would be wonderful.' My first – and only – 'espionage' operation would be over, I hoped, and I could relax and enjoy myself.

We heard Ada and Phoebe coming down

the hall to the lounge, so we scurried to opposite ends of the couch. In unison we picked up sections of the evening newspaper.

Ada went upstairs, but Phoebe brought her cup of tea into the lounge. Phoebe was a kind woman. She was worried sick about her sons, she'd brought strangers to live in her home, and she was considerate of Dellaphine and Madeleine. Would she really disapprove if Joe and I enjoyed a discreet affair in her house? Ada wouldn't care, and to hell with Henry.

Phoebe stirred her tea with a silver teaspoon monogrammed with an elaborate H, the initial of her last name. Earl Grey tea swirled around the rim of one of her bone china teacups. We never used either in our daily meals.

I guessed Phoebe was near fifty, but she seemed older to me. She wore her pre-war styled skirts below her knees and crimped her hair like she was still living in the thirties. She complained about all the changes brought about by the war, everything from married women leaving their children in day nurseries and going out to work, to servicemen wearing uniforms in church. She wanted her world to return to the way it was before the war. Most of us did not.

No, Phoebe was not a modern woman. She would be horrified if Joe and I did anything

166

more than hold hands under her roof. Most likely she'd evict us if she caught us. And then where would we go? Share an apartment? It would be impossible to find a decent one without producing a marriage certificate to a potential landlord. I doubted we could afford it, anyway. A two and a half room apartment ran to about ninety dollars a month. And I didn't know any woman who survived the damage to her reputation if the word got out she was shacked up. Some women thrived despite a non-conventional lifestyle, like Dora Bertrand, a lesbian who lived openly with her lover, but they were rare exceptions. Dora was a brilliant anthropologist critical to OSS's work in the Pacific. I wasn't.

Betty was at her accustomed place at her typewriter when I arrived at the office Friday morning. She looked like her old self. She'd repaired and polished her fingernails their usual bright red, and her hair was shiny, clean, and styled. But a different woman inhabited her body, a somber one, with her eyes hooded, concealing her feelings.

'Hi,' I said. 'I'm so glad you're here. How do you feel?'

'Tired,' she said. 'And a little scared. But I'm OK.'

'You follow the plan, and everything will

work out. Myrna and Lil will help you.'

'Myrna's moving out,' she said, 'getting her own apartment.'

I bet she was. And I wondered again what Myrna's 'job' with OSS was.

'And, listen, thanks,' she said. 'Thanks for everything. I was too upset to think. I'll do my best to keep myself together.' Resolutely, she inserted a dictation tape into her Dictaphone and settled the earphones over her head. She pulled paper, onion-skin, and carbon paper from her drawer and rolled it into her typewriter.

Don Murray appeared at my office door. 'Could you come down to my office, please, Mrs Pearlie, and bring your notebook with you?'

'Of course,' I said, grabbing my stenographer's pad and a pencil.

I knew the instant I walked into Don's office that something terrible had happened. Melinsky, in uniform, Don, and Max Corso, the head of the Italian desk for Special Intelligence, were all waiting for me.

'Sit down, please, Mrs Pearlie,' Corso said. He pulled the only comfortable chair in the office out for me. Don handed me a cup of coffee, a first. I steeled myself.

'Our operation has been cancelled, Mrs Pearlie,' Melinsky said.

'Why?' I asked, knowing they didn't have to tell me. I gripped the arms of my chair so

168

hard that my knuckles turned white with the effort. I was determined to behave professionally, even though my mind churned and my stomach cramped into the size of a walnut.

'Alessa Oneto is dead,' Corso said.

TWENTY-THREE

I struggled so hard to appear professional and controlled that I bit my tongue. I tasted the drop of blood in my mouth and pulled my handkerchief out of my sleeve to blot it quickly, so the men wouldn't see.

'What happened?' I finally asked.

'Here's what we know,' Melinsky said. 'Our man at Union Station reported that Alessa and her husband's secretary, Rossi, arrived from New York yesterday afternoon and took a taxi to the Mayflower. As we discussed earlier we kept our distance and didn't tail them any further.'

'Our agent in the DC Police called me this morning,' Corso said, 'to tell me that a Sicilian national killed herself at the Mayflower Hotel. It was Alessa Oneto.'

Impossible. Alessa would not kill herself, I thought, but I didn't say so out loud. I didn't want the men to think I was another hysterical woman.

'How do they know it was suicide?' I asked instead.

'When Count Oneto woke up, Alessa was

dead in their bed; had been for several hours, apparently,' Don said. 'The DC Police haven't gotten much information out of the husband, he's been distraught. But the mother-in-law said much of her laudanum and Nembutal was missing. The two women shared a bathroom, so Alessa could have taken a handful of pills as she was preparing for bed. And the secretary, Rossi, said that Alessa seemed depressed on the train ride home.'

I didn't believe a word of it.

'There will be an autopsy and an inquest, of course,' Melinsky said. 'The police have searched the crime scene and lifted fingerprints from the medicine bottles. We'll find out the results from our agent.'

I framed my words so I'd seem unemotional about Alessa's death. 'Colonel Melinsky,' I said, 'it seems unlikely to me that Alessa Oneto killed herself. She was dedicated to this operation. If she came back from New York with the information promised by her asset, couldn't that have had something to do with her death?' I allowed myself to use the word I had been thinking all along. 'Couldn't she have been murdered? What about the FBI? Aren't they involved in this, since Alessa was a refugee?'

'Murder is unlikely,' Don said. 'An FBI agent was on the scene with the police, but he concluded Alessa's death was a suicide and left the case to the police to wrap up.'

'How could he be so sure?'

'Louise,' he said gently, 'laudanum tastes vile in an amount large enough to kill. She wouldn't have swallowed anything that tasted of it by accident. And if she'd been forced, there would have been evidence of it on her body or at the scene. The FBI concluded she took the laudanum willingly and went to bed as she usually did.'

'There's nothing OSS can do?'

'We have no authority to conduct a domestic murder investigation,' Corso interrupted. 'And we can't allow the police to know that Alessa was involved in an OSS operation. Police headquarters leaks like a sieve, and crime reporters would crawl all over it. If we tell the police that Alessa was involved with OSS, we might as well broadcast it on the radio. We have no choice but to turn over the file to the Office of Naval Intelligence. The Port of New York is their territory. Without Alessa OSS has no dog in this hunt.'

Melinsky nodded to the other two men and they left the room, leaving me with my handler – if he was still my handler.

'I know you had a personal relationship with Alessa Oneto,' Melinsky said.

'I did. We were friends before all this.'

'You do understand that OSS involvement must stop now?'

'Yes, I see that.'

Melinsky leaned back in his chair and pulled out his cigarette case.

'I would like one of those,' I said. 'I don't usually smoke, but...'

'Of course,' he said, handing me a Sobranie, and then lighting it for me.

I inhaled. The cigarette had more depth than a Lucky Strike; the smoke carried exotic flavors. I could see why people who could afford it splurged on them.

'But,' Melinsky continued, 'we need to wrap up a couple of loose ends.'

So Alessa's death was a loose end.

'You will need to go on to your knitting circle tonight,' he said. 'How you'll behave will depend on whether the news of Alessa's death makes the afternoon papers. We will meet here before you leave work today. If her death is in the papers, with a picture, you will of course discuss it this evening. If not, you will simply wonder where she is.'

I wished acting were included in my training at 'The Farm'. This was going to be challenging, to say the least.

'"Anne" will be at the knitting circle, too.'

'My babysitter?' I said. 'Why?'

'Because we don't know for sure what happened to Alessa. We don't know if an enemy agent might be watching you, or if you've been tailed. For the same reason, Jack will pick you up at the designated rendezvous as usual. Instead of bringing you to me, though, he'll drive around a bit to make sure no one is following you, and then drop you near your boarding house.'

'OK,' I said.

Melinsky rested his elbows on the desk and leaned forward. 'Louise,' he said, 'be careful for a few days. Watchful. When you're not at work stay at home. Until we see the final police report on Alessa's death. If you need to talk to me, tell Don and he'll arrange a meeting.'

'Certainly,' I said.

My foray into espionage was over. And I'd never see Alessa again.

I made it to the ladies restroom, thankfully empty, before my bowels turned to water and I permitted tears to form and fall. Afterwards I sat on the toilet seat, coiled into a tight ball with my feet resting on the edge of the toilet bowl, my arms around my knees and my head down. I needed a few minutes to pull myself together.

I was presentable, I thought, when I returned to the office. My girls thought otherwise.

'Are you OK?' Ruth asked. 'You look so pale.'

'I'm fine,' I said.

'Don't get whatever illness Betty had,' Brenda said.

Betty stiffened and tears came into her eyes, but she lowered her head over her typewriter and the other two girls didn't notice.

I went to my desk and sorted index cards with a vengeance. Hours would pass until I spoke to Melinsky again, and more hours until I went to my knitting circle to play my part. I desperately wanted this day to end.

I was sure Alessa hadn't committed suicide. It made no sense at all to me. I'd never noticed any despondency in her, or fear, which would have led to such a despairing act. She'd been murdered, I knew it, because of the information she'd brought back from New York. I doubted if Melinsky would even tell me what the police concluded after their investigation. Why would he? I was a cut-out. The less I knew, the better.

Melinsky and I met over a weak cup of coffee in the OSS cafeteria after most of the staff had gone home for the day.

'It's in the papers,' Melinsky said, handing me copies of the *Herald* and the *News*. 'There's a photograph of her, and she's identified as Countess Oneto.'

I unfolded the *Herald*. Alessa's 'suicide' was reported below the fold on the front page. This would be all we'd talk about at the knitting circle tonight.

'Memorize what's in these articles,' Melinsky said. 'You should know nothing other than what's in the newspapers. And what all the other knitters knew about Alessa from the evenings you spent together.' Like how Alessa had disguised herself as a poor refugee. I knew that would come up in the conversation tonight.

I committed the brief paragraphs to memory and gave the papers back to Melinsky.

'Play it by ear,' Melinsky said. 'You're as shocked as anyone and as surprised that Alessa was a countess as the rest of them.'

'Of course,' I said.

Melinsky reached his hand over the table, and I took it. I barely felt his grip; I was still numb with shock.

'It was good to know you,' he said. 'Perhaps we will cross paths again.'

Melinsky left, giving me a quick smile before he went out the door. I was alone except for a grizzled colored man mopping the floor. I wanted to throw my coffee cup at the wall and pound the scarred wooden table with both fists, but instead I rubbed my aching temples.

'Bad day, miss?' the colored man said as he came near with his mop.

'Awful,' I said. 'Awful.'

He paused, then put a wiry hand on my shoulder. 'Remember, miss,' he said. 'The Good Lord won't send you nothin' you can't handle. You be stronger than you know.'

'Thanks,' I said. He patted my shoulder and moved away.

I was only being respectful to him. In less

than a year I'd moved so far from my Southern Baptist roots that I well knew He could send me plenty of trouble I couldn't handle. Look at what horrors went on in this world already! Depression, world war, millions of innocent people dead and displaced. Innocent dreams shattered forever. If God planned to intervene, He was taking his time about it. No, it was up to us humans to cope with this Armageddon all by ourselves. And it wasn't clear yet that the good guys would win.

Alessa's death was a tiny pebble cast into a maelstrom of horror, but it was enough to overwhelm me.

'Dearie,' Phoebe said, 'are you all right? You look ill.' She and Dellaphine had *The Boston Cooking School Cookbook* out, poring over recipes at the kitchen table, planning menus for the week ahead. Including Thanksgiving.

I'd learned at OSS to tell as close to the truth as possible when lying was necessary. The fewer falsehoods to get caught in, the better.

'I'm terribly upset,' I said. 'A friend of mine has died, and the police are saying it's suicide. I can't believe it.'

'A good friend? Someone we know?' asked Dellaphine.

'No,' I said. 'A woman from my knitting group.'

177

'I'm so sorry, Louise,' Phoebe said. 'Let me fix you some tea.' I would have liked a shot of Mr Holcombe's bourbon, but figured it would be unwise to ask for it.

'That would be lovely,' I said.

The kettle came to a full head of steam quickly. Phoebe poured hot water into her china teapot – no newfangled tea bags for her – and let it steep. Soon I was sipping strong Earl Grey with honey and milk while watching Phoebe and Dellaphine sort through recipes. I felt calmer now that I was home.

Funny how I'd lived here at 'Two Trees' for less than a year, but I already thought of it as home.

We were a solemn group that gathered in the women's club room of the Union Methodist Church that evening. The sexton had stoked the coal fire in the pot-bellied stove for us, so at least our bodies were warm, if not our spirits.

Our group was small, too. Me; Laura; Pearl of the gorgeous mink coat; another regular, Miriam, an older woman who rarely said much; and Anne, my babysitter.

'Hi, everyone,' she said. 'I'm Anne. I heard about this group from my landlady. I hope you don't mind if I join you tonight?'

'Of course not,' Laura said. 'The more the merrier.' Then she checked herself. 'Though

I'm afraid we're not very merry tonight.'

'Oh, why not?' Anne said as she pulled her project out of a deep carpet-bag, a heavy khaki sweater and a tangle of knitting needles and yarn. There'd be a standard issue .45 caliber Colt revolver in the bottom of that bag, too. It would be much more effective than my knife, which I still carried in my pocketbook. So silly for me to have made so much of my time at 'The Farm'. My assumption of the title 'agent' embarrassed me now. I'd accomplished nothing and wouldn't have the chance again.

'One of our regulars died,' Pearl said.

'Oh no!' Anne said. 'How?'

'It was in all the afternoon papers,' Laura said. She was working on a pair of the fingerless gloves from the pattern she'd given us last week. 'She killed herself!'

'How awful,' Anne said.

'She was a refugee from somewhere in Italy,' Pearl said, pulling off her wide gold bracelet with the diamond clasp so she could knit without impediment and dropping it carelessly into her pocketbook.

'You knew her the best,' Laura said, turning to me. 'You lunched together a few times, didn't you?'

'Yes,' I answered. 'She was a very sweet woman. I'm shocked that she'd do such a thing.'

'Perhaps she couldn't bear being away

179

from home any more,' Anne said.

'You know the really crazy part?' Laura said.

Here it comes, I thought.

'She was a countess! And rich! She and her husband lived in a suite at the Mayflower. The picture in the paper showed her wearing a ball gown and a tiara!'

'She pretended to be poor when she was with us,' Pearl said. 'She must have bought the clothes she wore at some thrift shop. Why do you think she did that, Louise?'

'I have no idea,' I said. 'But I can guess. So she could be herself, not get special attention?'

'It was a disguise,' Miriam said.

My heart began to pound. Surely this mousy woman had no idea of Alessa's plan.

'A disguise?' Pearl asked. 'What do you mean a disguise?'

'She didn't want to be herself,' Miriam said. 'She was ashamed.'

'What on earth of?' Laura asked.

'Of being a wealthy foreigner, with nothing to do but live in a fancy hotel safe and sound, while our boys are fighting for her country. It would shame me, I can tell you.'

I exhaled slowly in relief.

'It's a sad story,' Anne said. 'I'm sorry for her.'

'And I just dropped a stitch,' I said. The silence that followed told me we were all remembering how Alessa always repaired my mistakes.

'Hand it over,' Anne said. 'I can fix it.'

After two hours of a lot less conversation than usual, we began to pack up our work bags.

Anne turned to me. 'I heard there is a late night market around here,' she said. 'Do you know where it is?'

'I do,' I answered. 'You need to go up to I Street, turn left on Twenty-First, cross Pennsylvania Avenue, and the Western Market is a block down on the right. I'll walk with you.'

'I don't want to trouble you,' Anne said.

'It's no trouble. I'd like to get some air.'

The two of us walked together to the market. Anne showed no signs of being a trained secret agent, but then she wouldn't have been a very good one if she had, would she?

Once inside Anne guided me down the canned food aisle, which was sparsely stocked to say the least. People must be stocking up for Thanksgiving, less than a week away now. Without a word Anne shoved open the back door for me. Jack waited in an idling car, one I hadn't seen him drive before, and I climbed in next to him. Anne shut the door. Once back inside she'd do some shopping as cover, then leave with a bag of groceries and her knitting bag. I wouldn't see her again.

'I'm to drive you around a bit, then take you home,' Jack said.

'Could you go down Johnson Street, please?'

'I suppose so,' Jack said.

'Here,' I said. 'Stop here.'

'Ma'am, I'm not supposed to stop...'

'Damn it, Jack! Stop!'

Hearing me swear must have impressed him, because Jack pulled into a parking spot right in front of a late-night liquor store lit up by a gold neon Martini glass, complete with a green olive and a red swizzle stick.

'I'll be right back,' I said.

Inside, the man behind the counter looked shocked to see a woman alone. I couldn't have cared less.

'Give me a pint of Gordon water and a pint of vermouth, please,' I said and handed him a five-dollar bill.

He filled my order in disapproving silence. I put both the bottles, wrapped in newspaper, into my knitting bag.

Jack didn't say a word when I got back into the car, and I wasn't in the mood to chat.

A few minutes later he dropped me a few doors down from 'Two Trees' and tipped his hat to me. 'Good evening, ma'am,' he said.

I doubted I'd see Jack again, and he'd been perfectly nice to me, so I found my manners. 'Thank you, Jack,' I said. 'For everything.'

Thank God no one was downstairs. I

wasn't in any mood to make pleasant conversation. I slipped up to my bedroom and changed into a new pair of flannel pajamas, the ones with the thin blue and purple stripes. Then I poured what I estimated was a jigger of gin into my tooth glass and sprinkled some vermouth on it. I hid the bottles in my dresser, climbed into my bed, and sipped on my Martini. I was a grown woman and this was my home, and I was going to have a drink if I wanted one!

TWENTY-FOUR

When I slept, I slept badly. Most of the night I thought about Alessa, but not before I had the good cry I'd smothered all day. Had Alessa really killed herself? Had she been murdered? If she was murdered, was her death related to her contact with OSS, or was it personal? Since the investigation of her death was in the hands of the DC Police, would I ever know what actually happened to her? What about her asset – was he safe? Had she picked up the name of the quisling that OSS needed from her asset when she was in New York, and if so, where was it? According to Melinsky and Corso, this was no longer OSS's business, and so no longer mine.

I got out of bed early Saturday morning and went into the kitchen to make biscuits, killing time before the morning papers arrived. The biscuits came out of the oven golden and flaky. Their homely odor lured my housemates into the kitchen from all directions, except for Ada, who would still be sleeping after her usual late night gig with

184

the Willard house band.

The papers came. I commandeered *The Washington Post*. It was less likely to have grisly pictures in it. Although I figured the Mayflower security staff would have kept the most perverse of the newspaper photographers out of the hotel. I was relieved to see that the picture of Alessa was the same as Friday's, a genteel portrait of her with a tiara, not one of her body twisted up in her sheets in a nightdress, with dead eyes staring. Tears began to form, but I ruthlessly suppressed them.

The article added little to what I already knew. Alessa was an exiled Sicilian countess who lived with her husband Count Sebastian Oneto and his mother in the Mayflower Hotel. She'd recently returned from a visit to a friend in New York City. The count's private secretary, Orazio Rossi, accompanied her on the train while going to the city on a short holiday. Everyone who knew the Countess, from the doorman to the waiters, said she was kind and unpretentious. According to the family's maid, interviewed through a cascade of tears, she helped prepare breakfast and lunch for the family. She even attended a church knitting circle to make gloves and socks for servicemen overseas.

This was new. So her family knew about the knitting circle. But did they know she attended it disguised as a poor refugee and never mentioned her family?

The police at the scene said the appearance of the countess's corpse was consistent with suicide. The countess shared a bathroom with her mother-in-law, who possessed a quantity of Nembutal and laudanum, with enough missing to ensure death. Blood and tissue samples would be taken to verify the cause of death. Final dispensation rested on the coroner's report.

Although the countess did not appear despondent in the days before her death, Police Sergeant So-And-So, the senior officer on the scene, observed: 'Sometimes people snap, especially in these difficult times.'

He added: 'Laudanum tastes so dreadful that it was unlikely the Countess would take so much by accident.'

Count Oneto was said to be distraught and under a doctor's care. I felt for him. And I felt for myself, too, wondering how I could live with all the unanswered questions I had about Alessa and her death. Deep down, though it made little rational sense, I still didn't think she'd killed herself.

For the rest of the day I kept myself as distracted as possible with chores. I taught Henry how to use the washing machine and how to hang his clean clothes on the clothesline so they would need as little ironing as possible. I helped Phoebe polish the silver she wanted to use for Thanksgiving dinner. I wrote a letter to my parents – always a challenge because there was so little of my life I wanted to tell them about – and one to Rachel in Malta. I helped Ada twist her hair into a new style before she and her clarinet went off to work at the Willard Hotel.

And, of course, I was supposed to go out with Joe, an occasion that would have left me giddy with anticipation if I wasn't grieving for Alessa. And, yes, I was grieving, both for her untimely death and the failure of our operation. I fretted over all those convoys steaming across the Atlantic, vulnerable to sabotage and submarines.

Joe and I found ourselves alone in the lounge for a few minutes during the late afternoon.

'Are you all right?' he asked. 'You're not yourself today.'

I told as much of the truth as I could. 'Not really,' I said. 'One of the women I knit with killed herself on Thursday.'

'Oh, Louise, how awful!'

'Even more surprising, she disguised herself as a poor refugee, when she was really a countess. So she could have some anonymity, I think.'

'Were you friends?'

'We had lunch a couple of times. I liked her.'

'Do you have any idea why she'd do such a

thing?'

'No idea. I'm sure the Sunday papers will be full of it again tomorrow.'

'If you don't want to go out tonight, I understand. But you've got to eat dinner.'

I realized he was right. I'd had nothing but a cup of coffee and a biscuit all day. 'I would like to have dinner, if you can put up with me.'

'Let me see what I can find. Where's to-day's newspaper?'

'Childs would be fine, really!' Restaurants were packed on Saturdays, as most boarding houses didn't serve meals on the weekends. Many, like Betty's, offered no meals at all, leaving their residents to subsist on cafeteria and diner food.

I tried to cheer myself up by wearing my new suit dress again, and I must say it was a becoming color. Joe borrowed Phoebe's car, and I noticed that I felt quite natural sitting next to him in the passenger seat while he drove.

We arrived at the nearest Childs, the one near the White House and the Willard Hotel, early enough to get a table for two in a corner. I didn't want Joe to spend a lot of money, so I ordered a beer instead of a cock-tail and chicken croquettes with mashed potatoes and carrots. Joe ordered a beer, too, and a hot open-faced chicken sandwich with French fries. Our drinks and meals came right away. I found I was hungry after all. Halfway through our meal Joe ordered us each a second beer.

'I read the article in the newspaper about your friend,' Joe said. 'She was a Sicilian countess? If you don't want to talk about it, I understand.'

'Yes, Alessa Oneto was her name. I didn't know her last name until today. Or that she was a countess.'

'Sicily is an odd little island.'

'What do you mean?'

'It's been ruled by so many different nations that the country has been unstable for centuries.'

'I didn't know that,' I said.

'Let's see,' Joe said, ticking countries off on his fingers. 'Greece, Rome, the Goths, Byzantium, the Arabs, the Germans, the French, the Duchy of Naples, Spain. It wasn't until a hundred years ago that Italy took possession of Sicily, and Sicily considered the Italians another bunch of foreigners lording it over them. The Mafia came to power because Sicilians didn't trust their rulers, whoever they were, so they counted on a local organization to keep order.'

'Then Mussolini threw out the Mafia.'

'Yes,' Joe said, 'and most of them emigrated to America.'

'Lucky us.'

'Dessert?'

'No, thanks. Would you mind if we went home?'

'Of course not,' Joe said, gesturing for the bill. 'Sure you don't want to duck into Lafayette Park for a few moments of privacy?'

I had to laugh, remembering our experience with the auxiliary policeman.

'I'd be tempted,' I said, 'but it's Saturday night. Every park in the city is crawling with military policemen, DC police, and those damned civilian cops.'

When we arrived back at 'Two Trees' Phoebe met us at the door.

'There's a young gentleman here to see you,' she said to me. 'He's been waiting in the lounge for an hour. He's a foreigner – Italian, I think.'

The young gentleman, a dark, well-dressed man, rose to his feet as Joe and I entered the lounge. He bowed slightly and took my hand. He'd be really handsome, I thought, if he didn't slick his hair down with brilliantine.

'Mrs Pearlie,' he said, 'I apologize for intruding without an introduction. I am Orazio Rossi, Count Sebastian Oneto's private secretary.' I was taken aback. How had this man found me? What did he want?

'Oh,' I said, finding my voice. 'I'm pleased to meet you. This is my friend, Joe Prager.'

'I'll leave you two in private,' Joe said,

guessing we would be talking about Alessa.

Rossi was still standing.

'Please have a seat,' I said, gesturing to Phoebe's battered divan. I took the other end.

'As I'm sure you realize,' Rossi said, 'I am here because of the death of the Countess Alexandra Oneto.'

'How did you know who I am and where to find me?' I asked.

'I pray you do not object, but I questioned the minister at the church where you attended the knitting circle with Countess Oneto. He gave me your name, and the names of the other women there.'

'Oh,' I said. 'I don't mind.' As long as my cover wasn't blown. Or Alessa's.

'The Countess often spoke of how much she enjoyed your company, indeed, the companionship of all the women. And I understand you sometimes lunched together.'

'I liked her very much.'

'The Count and Countess know so few people here. As you can imagine, her death has desolated the family. The Count is holding a small reception in his wife's memory tomorrow. I hope I can prevail upon you to attend. It would mean so much.'

I hesitated. Melinsky and Corso had told me my involvement with this operation ended Friday after the knitting circle met. But wouldn't it look odd if I didn't attend?

And what if Alessa had brought back the information we so desperately sought from New York, and what if she hadn't committed suicide? Suddenly, I wanted to get into that apartment and meet her husband and mother-in-law. Maybe then I would have some idea of her mental state before her death.

'Two other ladies from the knitting group, Mrs Laura Coleman and Mrs Pearl Hamilton, have accepted. And there will be friends from the hotel and some staff also.'

I couldn't consult Melinsky before Monday. Surely, he would want me to accept?

'I'm honored to be invited, and I will be happy to attend,' I said.

'Thank you,' Rossi said, 'it will mean so much to the Count. I will see you tomorrow at one o'clock. Apartment Five-One-Eight at the Mayflower Hotel. If you enter through the residents' entrance, the doorman, Hays, will give you directions.'

I walked him to the door. Rossi shook my hand again and inclined his head in a gesture that reminded me of Rex Harrison in *Major Barbara*. He really was quite good-looking.

I found Phoebe and Joe in the kitchen drinking tea.

'Who was that young man, dear?' Phoebe asked.

'You remember the Countess who died, the woman who was in my knitting circle?'

'Yes,' she said. 'It was in the paper. She

committed suicide, didn't she?'

'Supposedly,' I said. 'Anyway, that was the Count's private secretary. He invited me to a reception in her memory tomorrow.'

'You accepted?'

'I did. I liked her, and I feel sorry for her husband.'

'So you've been invited to swell the crowd,' Joe said.

His cynicism surprised me. 'I guess so,' I said. 'But I don't mind.'

'He was a handsome young man, I must say,' Phoebe said.

'Typical aristocrat's flunkey,' Joe said. 'Europe is congested with them. At least, it was before the war. Good families, good education, no money. Live their whole lives handling the affairs of those who do.'

Joe spoke as though he was familiar with Rossi's life situation, and that reminded me that I knew absolutely nothing about Joe that he hadn't told me himself, and even that was very little. It was a good thing I didn't want to marry him. He could be anyone.

TWENTY-FIVE

Sebastian Oneto greeted me at the door of his apartment. Despite the sunglasses he wore to disguise his swollen eyes, I could see the evidence of sleepless nights in his pinched face. Though immaculately dressed in black suit and tie, Oneto was thin and stooped, looking older than I pictured him. Although that could be the result of grief, too.

I took his hand. 'I'm Louise Pearlie. I'm so sorry about Alessa. I liked her very much.'

'She was fond of you also,' Oneto said. 'Thank you for coming.'

It was a small group that gathered in the Oneto apartment. I recognized Rossi, of course, and Sebastian's mother, Lucia. She looked too young to be a dowager anything. She must have married young, because I doubted she was out of her forties yet. She was talking to C.J. Mack, general manager of the Mayflower, whom I recognized from newspaper photographs.

Two women about Lucia's age sat on the brocaded sofa, drinking tea; her friends, I

194

supposed.

Pearl, who must have been wearing every piece of jewelry she owned, along with a silk designer dress, stood at the window chatting with Rossi and Laura.

It was a pathetically small group to be mourning a woman as young and vibrant as Alessa, and I felt tears of my own well up. Sebastian noticed and turned away from me to hide his own emotion.

'Where is that girl!' Lucia said. 'The canapés should be served.'

'If you mean Lina,' Rossi said, 'she's still crying in her room.'

'Oh, I'll get them, then!' Lucia said, stubbing out her cigarette and moving toward the kitchenette.

'I'll help,' I said.

Inside the tiny kitchenette Lucia and I arranged the canapés, delivered from the hotel kitchen on a crystal plate. I could hear quiet weeping coming from behind a door to the maid's room.

'We could bring only one servant with us,' Lucia said, making no attempt to lower her voice, 'and Alessa insisted on Lina. She is not the one I would have chosen, but as always Sebastian submitted to Alessa's preferences.'

'Mrs Oneto...' I said, not knowing exactly what to call her.

'You may call me Lucia. I am a countess,

195

but that seems to mean little in your country.'

'Thank you. Lucia, do you really think that Alessa killed herself?'

'What other explanation could there be?' she said impatiently. 'She died in her sleep. Some of my laudanum and Nembutal pills are missing. She and I shared a bathroom, so she knew where to find them.'

'What I mean is,' I continued, 'she didn't seem despondent to me.'

'Who knows what goes on in another person's mind?' Lucia said. 'Alessa and I weren't intimate. I don't know what she might have been thinking.'

I felt it would be pushing it to question her any further. I longed to knock on Lina's door and talk to her, but I didn't see how I could do that without being noticed.

Lucia carried the canapés into the living room while I stacked cookies on another plate and snooped a bit. The tiny kitchen was between the maid's room and a dining room, no bigger than a breakfast room, really. The bedrooms and bathrooms must be on the other side of the living room, I thought, and the one door I noticed in the living room wall must lead to a hallway that linked the sleeping quarters.

The apartment looked spacious and luxurious to me, but it must have been much smaller than what the Onetos were accustomed to in Sicily.

I still heard weeping in Lina's room, so I took the plate of cookies into the living room myself. Sebastian still stood near the door, expecting more mourners, I supposed. I hoped some turned up. He looked like he needed sustenance, so I took the cookies over to him. He took one and nibbled on it.

'If we were in Palermo it would be different. Alessa had dozens of friends,' Sebastian said, as if apologizing for the size of the reception.

'I understand,' I said. 'It's wartime. Everything is different.'

'Your friend Mrs Coleman told me that Alessa wore old clothes to your knitting group. That sounds like her. She would want to be treated the same as the other women there. She must have changed somewhere, because she always left here in her own clothing.'

I wondered where Alessa had changed. 'She used a different name, too,' I said.

'Di Luca,' Sebastian said. 'Luca was her father's name.'

A knock sounded at the door, and Sebastian opened it.

Outside stood a short stocky man dressed in a cheap suit that didn't fit him. He was a laborer; the hands that held his hat were chafed and reddened from the scrubbing they received every day.

'Please come in,' Oneto said.

'I shouldn't,' the man said. He reached out a calloused hand to Oneto, who took it without hesitation. 'I'm Enzo Carini. I work in the hotel silver room. I ran a few errands for the Countess. I only want to pay my respects.'

'Thank you, Mr Carini,' Oneto said. 'You are welcome. Please do come in and have a cup of tea.'

Carini looked directly at the hotel manager, who nodded his permission.

Carini perched gingerly on the edge of a chair, looking uncomfortable and out of place. I brought him a cup of tea and a cookie, and he seemed relieved to have something to do with his hands.

Sebastian still stood alone next to the door, while the others in the room chatted. I couldn't bear to see him there, waiting for mourners who would never come. I joined him.

'You know,' Sebastian said, without any prompting, 'Alessa was rarely despondent, but she was quite somber when she returned from New York on Thursday.'

'Really? Why?'

'I don't know,' he said. 'It was as if she'd acquired a heavy burden.'

My heart raced. The name of the quisling! Alessa's asset had given it to her! So where was it?

'I should have paid more attention to her mood. But I assumed it was because of her brother. She was often quiet after seeing him.'

'Her brother?' I said. 'She had a brother?'

'Yes, a half-brother, Salvatore. It's one of those ridiculous open secrets that families like ours keep. Alessa's father had an illegitimate son when he was very young. Of course, he couldn't marry the girl, she was a peasant. But he kept in touch with the boy and visited him often with Alessa after his marriage. Later he helped him emigrate to the United States.'

'Alessa visited him secretly?'

'More or less. I was happy for her to see him. My mother, that's another matter. She is old-fashioned. She thought it appalling that Alessa recognized Turi.'

I laid a hand on his arm. 'Why don't you come sit down?' I said. 'I'll get you some tea.'

Sebastian smiled for the first time that afternoon. He looked much younger. 'I need fortification much stronger than tea,' he said. 'Later.' Then the smile vanished. 'You know,' he said, 'Alessa and I postponed having children because of the war. I regret that so much now.'

I was grateful for a knock at the door and to see Sebastian greet two couples near his own age. The women both embraced him, and the men, wearing black armbands, shook his hand warmly.

The swelling of the crowd gave me an opportunity to explore the apartment. I wanted to see how the bedrooms and bathrooms were laid out.

I went to Lucia's side and whispered to her, asking for the bathroom.

'Dear,' she said, nodding at the doorway to what I'd gathered was the bedroom hallway, 'go in there. The first bathroom you come to is mine. You are welcome to use it.'

I closed the door behind me, and the chatter of the reception faded into silence. I'd been correct; this was the bedroom hallway. All the immediate doors were open or ajar, which saved me the worry of opening them.

I peeked into the first room. Lucia's, obviously. It was crowded with furniture: a wardrobe, despite a large closet; a vanity; and a boudoir chair. The rose patterned bedspread matched the curtains, which matched the fabric on the boudoir chair, creating a garden of pink and green that would have given me a headache.

The bathroom that Lucia and Alessa shared was next door. I opened the medicine cabinet, and among the aspirin, tooth powder, and cold creams rested a full bottle of laudanum and a tin of Nembutal tablets. I assumed they replaced the ones the police must have taken for fingerprinting.

Next down the hallway was Sebastian and

Alessa's room. He hadn't cleaned out her things: they were strewn everywhere. She had an additional wardrobe, too. The door was open, revealing her clothing. A lacy negligee and matching dressing gown hung on a hook. Even her knitting basket sat on the floor next to the desk she and Sebastian kept in their room instead of a dressing table. Its walnut surface was piled with books of Italian poetry and literature. Her jewelry case lay open on the boudoir chair. She owned some lovely pieces. So she wasn't the victim of a robbery. It was unlikely that a burglar would force laudanum on her, anyway.

A quick search of the wardrobe and closet didn't turn up Alessa's 'thrift shop disguise'.

The men's bathroom was stark in comparison to the women's. The medicine cabinet contained only shaving equipment, aspirin, and tooth powder.

Unlike the others, Orazio's bedroom door was closed. I hesitated to open it. I told myself I was running out of time to pretend I was using the bathroom, but I finally did turn the doorknob. It was locked. Well, why not, I thought as I made my way back to the living room. Orazio wasn't a member of this family. It was reasonable for him to want some privacy.

Some of the mourners left the party. Enzo was gone, as was Mr Mack, the two women whom I'd assumed were friends of Lucia's, and Pearl. One of the younger men was pouring whisky into a highball glass for Sebastian, and I felt it was time for me to go.

I heard the clatter of crockery from the kitchenette and decided to make one last attempt to talk to Lina.

She stood at the sink, washing teacups, her eyes still red from weeping.

'Let me help you,' I said, picking up a dish towel to dry the cups.

She nodded, and I wondered how to begin the conversation, or whether Lina could even speak English. Lina solved that problem for me herself.

'I blame myself,' Lina said, in English I could barely follow. 'If I had not left the countess alone, perhaps she would not have done it. She was very quiet when she arrived home, but I hadn't had an evening off in three weeks, and no one else was home.'

I grasped at the straw she offered me. 'Alessa was alone? Are you sure?'

'Yes, of course. The countess arrived home in the late afternoon on Thursday. The dowager countess went to dinner with friends. Alessa, the count, and *Signore* Rossi ate a light supper, and then the men went to a speech given by Count Sforza.' Sforza was a former Italian foreign minister and leader of Italian anti-fascists abroad. 'The countess asked me if I'd like the evening off, and of course I said yes,' Lina continued. 'She said she didn't need me, she would go to the coffee shop for a sandwich and go to bed early.'

Interesting! The apartment had been empty for part of the evening. Had Alessa left the door locked or unlocked? Who had keys?

'It wasn't your fault,' I said. 'You couldn't possibly have known.' I patted her on the back, and she managed a slight smile.

This changed everything. Alessa had been alone for a few hours that night. I didn't care what the police thought – someone could have murdered her, perhaps overwhelmed her and forced her to take the laudanum and Nembutal. This had to be reported immediately to Melinsky and Corso.

I took my leave of Count Oneto and what guests remained.

Laura went down in the elevator with me brimming over with excitement. She'd known a countess, she'd gone to a reception at the Mayflower, and she couldn't wait to tell her friends. Of course, it was so sad about Alessa.

I called a taxi while Laura waited for the bus. An expense, but one I was willing to assume to avoid Laura's chattering and have time to think. Questions overwhelmed my ability to organize them.

Had Alessa killed herself? Everyone in the

household knew where Lucia's medications were. They were common drugs – Phoebe had prescriptions for both.

Had Alessa been murdered? If so, had her death involved our operation?

Why did Lucia dislike Alessa so?

What had happened in New York that had made Alessa despondent? Did it have anything to do with her asset, or was it personal? Was her half-brother involved?

If Alessa had returned from New York with the name of our quisling, where was it? Had the police and the FBI searched the apartment thoroughly? What were the results of their search and of the autopsy? If she had the name we needed I couldn't believe she'd commit suicide without delivering it to me.

What errands had Enzo Carini run for Alessa?

Where had Alessa changed into her thrift shop disguise?

Who could have entered the residential areas of the Mayflower without being questioned, and how? Why had Alessa let him in? Had she known him?

Had she been murdered? Was the Mafia involved?

There were way too many questions for me to answer. I was relieved I would be turning all this over to Colonel Melinsky tomorrow.

Colonel Melinsky was furious. So were Don

and Max Corso.

'What did you think you were doing?' Melinsky asked.

'I did what I thought—'

'You weren't supposed to think!' Don said. 'OSS had closed down this operation! We'd turned this over to the DC Police and the Office of Naval Intelligence. Didn't you understand that when we talked last week, or weren't you listening?'

'Of course I was listening,' I said, as calmly as I could manage. 'But—'

'There are no "buts" in espionage,' Melinsky said. 'Following orders is crucial. You have no idea – damn it, one of the other guests at the apartment could have been an agent. You might have blown your cover! This is what happens when a half-trained person exceeds her assignment!'

Corso cleared his throat. 'The Coroner's Office has issued a certificate of suicide in Alessa Oneto's death. Do you think you know better than the DC Police and the Coroner?'

'Excuse me,' I said. 'What was I supposed to do? I couldn't ask you. I made a decision.'

Melinsky fumbled for his cigarettes, and I noticed his gold ring with the Rurik coat of arms. His English was so good that I'd almost forgotten he was a Russian nobleman.

While Melinsky lit his cigarette I had time

to compose myself. The last thing I'd expected when I met with him this morning was a dressing down. I'd actually thought Melinsky, Don, and Max Corso, would be pleased with the information I brought them, the evidence that Alessa Oneto could have been murdered, that her death might have had something to do with her bringing back the name of our Mafia sleeper. I was wrong.

'You should have declined the invitation to the reception and informed me of it this morning. That's all.'

I could not believe my ears. I wasn't supposed to collect crucial information that might still lead to our sleeper? What nonsense! What idiocy!

But I held my tongue. I'd learned years ago to keep my mouth shut. My bosses, Melinsky, Corso, even Don, were important men. I was a female file clerk. Arguing with them wasn't an option if I wanted to keep my job. And I did want to keep it, even if I had to wire my mouth shut.

'I apologize,' I said.

Melinsky exhaled a puff of smoke. 'I know you believed you were doing the right thing,' he said, some of his anger dissipating. 'I understand that.'

Did all this mean Melinsky would do nothing with the information I'd gathered from the reception? I found it hard to believe he would consider anything else other than delivering it straight to the FBI. It was unconscionable. Still I kept my mouth shut.

'I'm afraid this requires disciplinary action,' Don said.

Oh no!

'Corso and I agree,' Melinsky said.

'Suspension for insubordination for the rest of the week, without pay,' Don said. 'You will, of course, return to your job on Monday. You are an excellent clerk, and we need you here.'

Filing papers. Typing index cards. Good to know I excelled at that. I felt like a dependable plow mule.

'You may tell the girls in your office and anyone else who asks that you've been assigned to another special project,' Don said. 'We don't want them to know you've been disciplined. That might weaken your authority.'

'The suspension will be between the four of us,' Melinsky added.

But it would be recorded in my personnel file, a strike against me if I applied for a promotion or permanent employment after the war.

On my way back to the office my anger built to near explosion levels and my stomach cramped until it felt like a tennis ball lodged in my abdomen.

My refuge, the ladies' bathroom, was

empty. I took my usual reflective position on a toilet, my legs drawn up, my feet resting on the seat, and my head on my knees. But I didn't cry. Instead I beat on the wooden stall partition, with both hands, livid with anger. Who the hell did those three men think they were, to berate me, to suspend me, for taking a little initiative! What I reported to them this morning was valuable and important. Following up on it might save lives. I bet they'd figure out a way to get some of what I'd learned to the ONI, and guess who would get credit for it! Not me! What could you expect from someone like Melinsky, a man whose family owned serfs!

Damn Don! He wouldn't have dared suspend me if our workload hadn't slacked off!

I'd been suspended for insubordination! Even though I didn't have to admit it to any-one, a black mark would stay on my record, harming my chances for promotion. I'd be sorting index cards for the rest of the war, however long it lasted.

I stalked down the hallway to my office, keeping my eyes averted so I didn't have to acknowledge anyone, even Dora, who passed by me with a stack of books and papers and a pencil stuck behind her ear and one in her mouth.

Betty was the only one of my girls in the

office.

'Good morning,' she said. 'Ruth and Brenda have gone for coffee. They should be back soon. How was your weekend?'

Had I had a weekend? I almost didn't remember; it seemed like a month ago.

'Not so great,' I said. 'A woman I knew died. I went to a reception in her memory on Sunday.'

Betty turned to me, wiping the carbon from her hands with the damp cloth she kept on her desk.

'I'm so sorry. Who was she? Someone I know?'

'You probably read about her in the newspaper,' I said. 'She was the countess who died in her apartment in the Mayflower. I knew her from a knitting group we were in together. Except I didn't know she was a countess. She didn't tell us.'

Why was I telling Betty this? Why didn't I say, sure, I had a swell time over the weekend, went out drinking and jitterbugging like a normal government girl? Then I remembered my social niceties.

'And how was your weekend?' I asked Betty.

She instantly brightened in that all too familiar way. 'I had the nicest time,' she said. 'I went out with a swell guy.'

The one thing that could distract me from my pity party was the idea that Betty already had a new boyfriend. The girl was incorrigible.

'Don't look at me like that,' she said, reading my expression. 'He's not like the others.'

'Does he wear a uniform? Is he about to be sent overseas? Is he lonely?' That was unkind and cynical, but I couldn't help myself in the mood I was in.

Betty flushed. 'I don't blame you for being annoyed, but Ralph is different. For one thing he's a policeman, a lieutenant. He's pretty old – over thirty. He's not in the Army because he's Four-F.'

'Where did you meet him?' Some bar, I assumed.

Betty's flush spread down her neck and chest. 'At the jail. He was so nice to me.'

This I could not believe. I rolled my eyes.

'Don't do that!' she said. 'His sister got in the same fix, so he understands! I've learned my lesson, I really have!'

'OK,' I said, 'all right. I'm sorry.' And I was. I should give the girl a chance to prove she'd grown up.

Ruth and Brenda arrived, refreshed by their cups of joe.

'Is there any coffee left in the cafeteria?' Betty asked.

'Plenty,' Ruth answered, pulling on her black sleeve protectors. 'It's the beginning of the week. You go on.'

'Can I bring you some, Louise?' Betty

asked.

'You look like you could use it,' Ruth said, studying my face.

All the coffee in the world couldn't make me feel better.

'Wait for a minute, Betty,' I said. 'I need to talk to you all for a few minutes.'

'That doesn't sound good,' Ruth said.

'Nothing catastrophic,' I said, 'but I've been assigned to a new project. Another private library that needs sorting for useful material. It's here in town, so I'll be around. Ruth, you'll be in charge. If you have any questions or problems, ask Joan Adams. General Donovan is still out of the country, so she has some free time.'

Ruth sighed. 'Nobody in this building listens to me the way they do to you,' she said. 'Not Dr Murray, not Mr Austine, not anyone. They make a mess of the files and reports, and we have to clean up after them.'

I hadn't realized I was such a martinet. I rather liked the idea. 'Look at it this way,' I said to Ruth, patting her on her arm, 'you'll have a chance to practice command.'

'When will you be back?' Betty asked.

'Monday next,' I said.

Then it struck me. I had a week off! I hadn't had so much free time in, what, almost two years, since I first went to work at the Wilmington Shipbuilding Company.

And since I'd worked for OSS I'd had

211

exactly one weekday free: the Fourth of July.

I would have preferred not to be disciplined, but now I could help Dellaphine cook Thanksgiving dinner. I could sit out on the porch, wrapped in a blanket, and read. I could make a war cake. I could catch up on my knitting ... and then I remembered Alessa and the injustice of letting the judgment of suicide stand. Maybe she had killed herself, but I wasn't convinced. She was in the midst of bringing OSS critical information about a sleeper, a *Mafioso*, based in the New York City docks. She'd returned from New York, and perhaps she'd already had the information she'd promised us! And she was alone in her apartment for several hours. Plenty of time for her to be overwhelmed by someone and forced to poison herself, and for the stage to be set to look like suicide.

By the time I got off my bus and walked into Dellaphine's kitchen I'd made a dangerous decision. I was going to spend most of this week probing Alessa's death on my own. I owed her that much. I would be very careful, and if I turned up anything suspicious, I'd take it straight to the DC Police, I vowed to myself.

If I stumbled upon evidence that OSS could use, like the name of our man, I would deal with that when it happened. I didn't want to lose my job, but with a suspension for insubordination on my record, I wasn't sure how secure my job was any more. I didn't trust Don's reassurances. When I got back on Monday I might find myself in the mimeograph room.

'What are you doing home this early? Don't you feel well?' Dellaphine said, folding a basket of towels at the kitchen table. She'd pulled them off the line, and they smelled of laundry detergent and autumn.

I pulled a towel out of the laundry basket and shook it out. 'I've been suspended, for a week, for insubordination.'

'My Lord, Mrs Pearlie, what did you do?'

'I argued with my bosses.'

'They was mens?'

'All three of them.'

I folded the towel the way Phoebe liked them, both edges toward the middle so it would hang neatly on a towel rod.

'I'm sorry,' Dellaphine said. 'Will this hurt your future?'

'I honestly don't know,' I said. 'But I might as well grit my teeth and go on. It's wartime. Who knows what's going to happen? I've decided not to worry about it and enjoy my week off.' A week off without pay. I could get through the month all right though. I saved some of each paycheck, even though the government urged us to spend every extra penny on war bonds.

'That's right,' Dellaphine said. 'Enjoy

yourself while you can. Get some rest.'

'I'm going to help you cook Thanksgiving dinner,' I said. 'I know that much.'

I made a Spam and mayonnaise sandwich for myself and took it and a glass of milk up to my bedroom. I needed to collect my thoughts and plan the next few days. I hoped to do my investigating as unobtrusively as possible. My job with OSS might be shaky, but I wanted to keep it if I could.

As I thought of losing my job, a ripple of apprehension cascaded into pure fear. I felt it physically, frigid hands grasping my spine and shaking cold shivers through me. What if I did lose my job with a black mark on my record? Dear heaven, I'd have to go back home to Wilmington and live with my parents! I'd become again the widowed daughter with no prospects. I couldn't bear it. My resolve ebbed away. Alessa was dead; nothing I could do would bring her back. If the police and the coroner's office had declared her death a suicide, why shouldn't I accept that? After all, I didn't know her all that well. And if OSS had turned over the files on Alessa and her asset to the Office of Naval Intelligence, who was I to challenge that decision? My brief spell as a cut-out and a couple of days at 'The Farm' did not make me a real OSS agent. Melinsky was right: I wasn't trained to deal with an operation this complex.

As I abandoned my plan I felt my panic slowly subside. I managed to eat my sandwich and drink my milk.

But my mind still churned with questions about Alessa's death. It wouldn't hurt to write down what I knew, would it? Organize my thoughts so I could put them behind me and move on? I got a notebook and pencil out of the top drawer of my dresser.

I began at the beginning.

I first went the knitting circle early in October. Alessa, dressed in her thrift shop clothing, was already a member.

This seemed important. She hadn't joined the circle in search of a contact within the government; she'd approached me when she'd learned I was a government girl. Not only that, she hadn't had the Mafia sleeper's name yet. First she'd needed to assure herself, and her asset, that the information could be passed to a responsible person safely.

Had Alessa picked up this name on her last trip to New York, shortly before her death? If so, where was it now?

And what about Alessa's illegitimate half brother? Was he her contact, or was he peripheral, someone she visited while in New York? Sebastian told me that they lived in a New York hotel for a time before moving to Washington. Alessa must have met dozens of people in the city, any one of whom could be her asset. I didn't see how I could find out, and besides, I didn't know her brother's name.

Alessa died sometime between 7 p.m. and 10 p.m. on Thursday night when she was alone in her apartment.

Had the DC Police verified Orazio, Sebastian, Lina, and Lucia's alibis? Had Alessa allowed someone to enter the apartment, who subsequently killed her and set up the scene to look like a suicide? How easy was it, anyway, to get into the residential side of the Mayflower? Was a doorman on duty twenty-four hours a day? I'd never been required to sign in when I visited Joan Adams; did Hays wave everyone upstairs?

Where did Enzo fit in? What kind of 'errands' had he run for Alessa? Where had she changed into her 'thrift shop disguise'? And, in a sudden burst of insight, I wondered if she'd disguised her identity with anyone other than our knitting group.

If Alessa had brought back the name of the sleeper from her contact in New York, where was it? If she was murdered, which I felt in my very bones she had been, had the murderer found it?

I went over my notes. I needed to talk to Enzo first; then I intended to verify alibis. As discreetly as possible, of course.

I wished I could get my hands on the police report. How much did Ralph the

216

policeman like Betty?

I caught myself in mid-speculation. OK, so I hadn't given up. I did not for one second believe Alessa killed herself. I intended to spend this week investigating her death. If I could solve her murder, perhaps that would lead me to the name of the sleeper before the next slow convoy left New York, or thousands of lives could be at risk.

'What did you do?' Ada asked.

'Stopped shuffling index cards and took some initiative,' I said, helping myself to a scoop of mashed potatoes and bacon before passing it down the table to Henry.

'I'm sorry, dear,' Phoebe said, to me, not Henry. 'I'm surprised your office could do without you.'

'It's just for a week. And I'm allowed to lie about it. I can say I'm working on a special project so as not to lose my influence over my staff,' I said.

Henry didn't voice his opinion of my suspension. I'm sure I wouldn't have appreciated it.

I'd already pulled Joe aside and told him.

'I knew you'd get in hot water one of these days,' he said, 'you're such a troublemaker.' He kissed me quickly, before anyone could see him.

'And I pride myself on keeping my mouth shut,' I said. 'Didn't follow my own advice.'

'You could visit your parents,' Phoebe said.

I loved my parents, I did, but the thought of going home for any length of time made me feel sick. And here I was taking chances that could spoil my life in Washington. Well, if I lost my government job, I'd move someplace cheaper than 'Two Trees' and wait tables at Childs. I wasn't going home to North Carolina, and I wasn't leaving the questions I had about Alessa unanswered. I was stuck on this lonesome road, as I'd heard Sister Rosetta Thorpe sing many times on Dellaphine's gospel radio station.

Before joining the others in the lounge, I sat on the worn needlepoint chair in the hall and took the telephone on my lap. First I called Betty. She sounded like her old self and was eager to help me after everything I'd done for her. She didn't question why I wanted to meet Ralph, but eagerly agreed to introduce us. She and Ralph were having lunch together tomorrow at a soda fountain near work. Why didn't I join them? Then I could ask him whatever I wanted.

I spent a few minutes plotting my strategy before calling the Mayflower Hotel and asking to be put through to the silver room. I'd never considered myself much of an actress, but the man who answered the phone fell for my story hook, line, and sinker.

'Enzo Carini isn't here,' he said. 'He works the day shift, eight to six.'

'You see,' I said, hoping I sounded like a young shop girl. I needed to stay as far under the radar as possible. 'He lent me a dollar at the bus stop today, and I want to pay him back, but I don't know his address or anything.'

'If it's not raining you'll find Enzo outside the servants' entrance around ten fifteen tomorrow smoking a cigarette,' the man said. 'That's our morning break time.'

As I hung up the phone and replaced it on the telephone table, I wondered if I should write down all the lies I was telling in case I lost track of them.

TWENTY-SIX

Enzo offered me one of his Camels, and I shook my head.

He lit his and inhaled deeply, stuffing his cigarette pack and matches back into the pocket of his filthy apron.

'I am sorry not to shake hands,' Enzo said, 'but as you see I am working.'

Silver tarnish and cleaning paste encrusted his hands, forearms, and apron.

'It's OK, of course,' I said. Then I plunged in. 'I was a friend of Alessa Oneto, the countess, and I don't believe for a minute she killed herself. I know this sounds ridiculous, but I'm asking some questions on my own. I'm on leave from my government job, and I'll get fired if anyone finds out I am doing this.'

'I know how to keep secrets,' he said. 'I won't tell anyone. I am also distressed over the Countess's death.'

'Would you mind telling me what "errands" you did for Alessa?' I asked.

'I failed her,' Enzo said, without answering my question.

'What do you mean?'

'She paid me three dollars a week, and I failed to see that she was in danger. I should have protected her.'

'I don't understand,' I said.

'It's the tradition of my people,' Enzo said. 'An obligation.'

I figured he referred to some Sicilian custom. I let it pass.

Enzo stubbed out his cigarette on the sidewalk. 'Come with me,' he said. 'I will show you something. But you must not speak of me to anyone, as I will not speak of you.'

'Of course, but won't you be late for work?'

'I will say I helped unload the vegetable truck. I'm a good worker; it will be all right.'

Enzo led me down a flight of stairs into the immense basement of the Mayflower Hotel, the invisible world behind the scenes of the elegant hotel. Immediately, I smelled onions browning, something chocolate baking, and meat sizzling, all melded into one delectable odor.

'Look,' Enzo said, 'the kitchens are on this level. You must see.'

He opened a double swinging door into chaos. The noise of the huge kitchen was deafening. Chefs in white toques issued orders to an army of kitchen workers uniformed in blue blouses and white bandannas. Pots and pans crashed and clanged. Smoke and flames roared from gas ranges and were then sucked into ducts overhead. Electric refrigerators that must have cost a fortune lined a back wall. I caught sight of the scullery as an aproned woman came through its door balancing a tall stack of dishes. Almost invisible through the steam, an army of dishwashers scrubbed plates, glasses, pots, and pans in sparkling stainless steel sinks. Whoever managed the Mayflower had the foresight to equip it before the war ended the manufacture of kitchen equipment.

On a table the size of my bedroom, lined with ice, the day's fresh food lay ready for preparation. Vegetables, eggs, chicken, lobster, even several haunches of beef, were waiting to be prepared. The chicken I'd had at Joan's apartment only a week ago had been cooked here, loaded into a dumb waiter, lifted to a holding scullery upstairs somewhere, then delivered, still piping hot, to me.

Enzo swung the door closed. He led me down another staircase, two stories under street level, into the sub-basement. Here the ceiling was criss-crossed with pipes and ducts in all sizes and colors. I could hear the steam engines of the boiler room roaring nearby.

We turned into a dimly lit hall off the stairway and into a locker room. Single electric bulbs hung from a low ceiling layered with a spiderweb of steel beams, ducts, and pipes.

We ducked around a bank of toilets, where several lockers stood out of sight of the main room.

'I found this locker for the countess,' Enzo said. 'So she could change into old clothes before she went out sometimes. She didn't like people to stare at her in the shops and on the street.'

'Enzo, can we possibly open this locker?'

'Of course,' he said as he twirled the combination lock.

Alessa's disguise hung on a single hook. The man's greatcoat, shiny with wear; two threadbare dresses; a single pair of down at the heel black shoes. A scarf and toboggan she'd knitted herself were shoved on to the only shelf. I felt my throat begin to close, then forced myself to remain calm. I searched every pocket and sleeve of the coat and dresses, even checked the clothing seams for signs they'd been ripped open and re-sewn. I examined the insteps and soles of the shoes for slits where a document could be hidden, taking advantage of what I had learned at 'The Farm'. I even found a use for my switchblade when I used it to pry apart the stitched brim of Alessa's worn felt fedora.

Alessa's knitting bag wasn't in the locker, of course; it was upstairs in her bedroom next to the desk. I'd seen it when I prowled the bedroom wing of her apartment during the memorial.

223

Her knitting bag. If she'd had a letter to give to me at the knitting circle, what better place to hide it than in the chaos of her knitting bag! I could have kicked myself for not having the brains to search it when I saw it!

I slammed the door of the locker shut. 'Damn it!' I said, under my breath.

'You are looking for something in particular?' Enzo said.

'Yes, I am,' I answered.

'Is it important?'

'Very.'

We stared at each other, both unsure if we should share what we knew.

'I think,' Enzo said, 'that you and I are very good at keeping secrets.'

'Yes,' I said. 'We are.' I took a deep breath. 'I'm a government girl,' I said. 'But I work for an important agency. Alessa Oneto promised us information that we never received. I want to find out what happened to her, but I want that information, too. And I'm not supposed to be doing this. I could lose my job if my bosses knew.'

Enzo nodded, reflecting on what I'd told him. He peered around the corner, making sure the locker room was empty. 'I am *Mafioso*,' he said.

My heart jumped into my throat, and my hand went to my mouth.

'Just a *piciotto*,' he said, 'very unimportant. Some of the hotel guests play the numbers, some desire companionship, you understand. The Countess wanted a quiet place to change her clothes, that was all. But two weeks ago my *capo* told me to watch over the countess, and that the request came from a friend in New York. As I already had a business relationship with Countess Oneto, I took special care.'

I was still reeling from Enzo's stunning admission that he was a member of the Mafia. I thought of the Mafia as gangsters wearing double-breasted pinstriped suits being escorted in handcuffs to jail by J. Edgar Hoover. Or lying on a bloody sidewalk outside an Italian restaurant somewhere riddled with sub-machine bullet holes. Enzo was a working man making a few bucks from hotel guests on the side.

'What did you find out?' I asked.

'Very little. Except one day I overheard one of the waitresses, who is engaged to one of my friends at work. She was in the silver room during a break and told her friend she saw the Dowager Countess Lucia Oneto take a diamond bracelet off her arm and give it to Orazio Rossi.'

'Really!' I said.

'Yes. They were having coffee in the quietest corner of the coffee shop. We all laughed, thinking this was of a sexual nature – you know, the dowager countess is still young and attractive – but I filed it away here,' he said, and he tapped his forehead. 'Now I wonder if I should have told my *capo*, if perhaps it relates to the countess's death.'

'You don't think she committed suicide either, do you?' I said.

'No, I don't,' he said. 'She made so many plans, you understand? People with plans for the future don't kill themselves. Now I must go. Can you find the way out? We should not be seen together.'

'Certainly,' I said. 'And thank you. If you remember anything else, would you call me?' I scribbled my phone number on his matchbox.

'Of course,' he said. 'Wait a few minutes after I leave, please? Less chance of us being seen together.'

I waited, stewing over everything I'd learned, and a few minutes later left the locker room, headed for the stairs.

'Who are you, and what are you doing here?' a deep voice called out from across the wide hallway. I turned to see a heavyset man with a frown on his face and his arms crossed.

He wasn't a kitchen worker or a security guard; he was wearing a quality suit and tie.

'I'm lost,' I said, the first words that came to my mind.

'Are you a guest? Did you get on the service elevator by accident?'

'Yes,' I said. 'That must be what happened.

So surprised to find myself here!'

'Didn't realize it wouldn't stop until you got to the basement, I bet.'

'That's right.' By now my mind was working. 'I'm not staying here, actually; I'm visiting my friend Joan Adams, who has an apartment in the hotel.'

He stretched out a hand to shake mine. 'I'm Fred Gleim,' he said, his frown morphing into a warm smile. 'I'm the Mayflower Hotel silversmith. Since you're already down here, would you like to see the silver room?'

'Oh, yes,' I said, gushing. Surely a visitor to the Mayflower would jump at the chance?

'Right this way,' he said, leading me down the long hall through yet another swinging door.

Inside the high-ceilinged room, big as the kitchens a flight above, overhead lights reflected off table after table, shelf after shelf, and row after row of silver plate. I was struck silent by the sight of hundreds of coffee pots, candlesticks, urns, serving pieces, champagne buckets, trays, compotes, and trays full of silverware, all burnished to gleaming.

Despite the size of the room it was claustrophobic without natural light. And the acid odor of silver polish was nauseating. I didn't know how the workers could bear it.

'Incredible sight, isn't it?' he said. 'We polish, repair, and re-plate all the hotel silver.'

At the back of the room, behind a counter, at least ten men, including Enzo, worked, polishing. No wonder he was filthy with tarnish.

'Must be worth a fortune,' I said.

'Indeed. We keep an eye on it, too, during parties and receptions so guests don't walk away with souvenirs. Once after a Christmas party a punch bowl disappeared! Still don't know how that happened. Teaspoons are impossible to keep track of, though. You'd be surprised how many rich and important people think it's OK to walk off with a silver spoon because they dined in the Presidential Restaurant and want a memento with the Mayflower emblem. We've lost four thousand spoons since the hotel opened,' he said.

'I can see that it would be tempting,' I said.

'We're hosting a USO fund-raising ball here after Thanksgiving,' he said. 'Will you be attending?'

'I'm afraid not.' I was eager to get away. Mr Gleim was very attentive, as I suppose he was required to be to hotel guests, but I was anxious to put some distance between Enzo, this hotel, and me before I ran into someone I knew. 'Thank you so much for the tour,' I said.

'You're welcome,' he answered, with a slight bow. 'Will you permit me to escort you to the correct elevator?' he asked.

'Please.'

★ ★ ★

The elevator door opened on the ground floor into the main lobby of the hotel. Even royalty, I thought, couldn't help but be impressed by the marble floors and sumptuous decor of the grand hotel. I found myself wishing I could go to a ball here.

I walked, with my best imitation of nonchalance, past the hotel candy kiosk, coffee shop, and cigar stand, terrified of running into Count Oneto, Lucia, or Rossi before finding myself on the street, running late for lunch with Betty and her policeman beau. Three full buses passed me before I broke down and hailed a cab. I swore that as soon as possible I would purchase a Victory bicycle. I was tired of standing on street corners waiting forever to travel a few blocks.

I met Betty and Ralph at a People's Drug Store soda fountain around the corner from OSS headquarters.

Betty's appearance surprised me. She'd buttoned her dress to the neck, and she'd switched her lipstick and nail polish color from fire engine to brick red. As for Ralph, he was at least thirty-five, with a patch of gray prominent in his buzz-cut dark hair. A big man, he was comfortable in his police sergeant's uniform, projecting an air of competence and reliability. He stood up politely and shook my hand when Betty introduced us. Was it possible that Betty had grown up and acquired a mature man as her new boyfriend? From the way Ralph looked at her, I figured he'd do about anything for her. I hoped so.

Ralph went to the counter to pick up our grilled cheese sandwiches and chocolate shakes. Betty leaned over to me and whispered, 'Isn't he wonderful?'

'Yes,' I said, 'wonderful.' Betty was a sucker for a man in uniform, but this policeman was a huge improvement over the boy soldiers and sailors she'd dated before. I hoped she had the sense to stick with him.

I worried about bringing two more people into my confidence, but I couldn't make any progress unless I did. Betty might be ditzy, but she'd worked long enough at OSS to understand secrecy, and Ralph was a policeman, for heaven's sake.

Ralph set our tray of food down on the table.

Don't tell any more lies than necessary, I reminded myself.

'You know I'm working on a special project this week,' I said to Betty.

She nodded. 'Sorting a private library,' she said.

'Yes,' I said, 'but there's something else I need to do this week, and Ralph, I need your help.'

'Depends on what you want,' Ralph said.

'Betty's vouched for you; she says you have OSS Top Secret Clearance. That's good enough for me.'

'A friend of mine died last Thursday night,' I said. 'Countess Alessa Oneto.'

'The woman who killed herself?' he said.

'You knew her?' Betty asked. 'A real countess?'

'We were in a knitting group together. And we didn't know she was a countess. I was very fond of her, and I don't believe she killed herself. I want to find out more about what happened.' Of course, I left out the part about how Alessa might have the key to preventing the destruction of American convoys loaded with millions of dollars' worth of critical supplies for the North African front. The first slow convoy was scheduled to leave the Port of New York next week.

'What can I do?' Ralph asked.

I dived right in.

'I'd like to see the DC Police case file on her death.'

I waited for Ralph to be shocked, insulted, or at least perturbed. Instead, he wiped his mouth and sucked down the last of his milkshake.

'Is the case open or closed?' he asked.

'Closed, I think. The coroner issued a death certificate.'

'Then sure, I can get you the file. Our

231

closed files are open to the public. The problem will be finding it. You should see our file room. Papers and files stacked everywhere. Those loathsome crime reporters paw through them and foul up the filing system.'

'Honey, I don't want the rest of my sandwich,' Betty said to him. 'Would you like it?'

'Thanks, baby,' he said. 'It's tongue and cabbage casserole at my boarding house tonight.'

'Ralph,' I said, 'I can't be seen at the police station. Could you possibly ... I mean it's a lot to ask, but...'

I waited again for what I was sure would be Ralph's objection.

'I'll bring it to you,' Ralph said, finishing the rest of Betty's sandwich. 'If I can find it, that is. Since the deceased was a real countess, one of the clerks might actually have filed it correctly by now.'

Ralph's hand reached for the tab. 'My treat. I get a discount.'

If Betty didn't marry this man, she was a fool.

'I eat breakfast at the café on the corner of Nineteenth and C, near the jail, every morning at seven thirty. Can you meet me there?' he asked.

Another long taxi ride, another dent in my savings.

'I'll see you there!' I said. 'I can't thank you

enough!'

'I'd do anything to make my Betty happy,' he said, 'as long as it's legal.' He leaned over and kissed her sweetly, and a slow flush climbed her neck into her face.

'Ain't she pretty?' he asked.

'Stop it!' Betty said. 'You're embarrassing me.'

I'd never seen Betty blush before, or be embarrassed either. It was a wonder.

Betty and I walked a few blocks together – she on her way back to work, and me to my bus stop. On the way she grabbed my arm and pulled me into an alley.

'What is it?' I asked.

She was as pale as she'd been flushed in the drug store after Ralph's compliment.

'Louise,' she said, 'you've been married. Is it true, do you think, you know, that a man...' She hesitated.

'Spit it out, Betty,' I said.

She lowered her voice even further. 'That a man can tell if a woman's not a virgin.'

I restrained myself from laughing out loud only because Betty looked so troubled. 'I promise you, Ralph does not expect you to be a virgin!'

'You don't think so?'

'Honey, you met him when you were in jail! For possibly having venereal disease!'

'I told him that the guy was lying because I wouldn't sleep with him.'

I put an arm around her shoulder. 'Betty, dear one, Ralph doesn't believe that for a minute.'

'And he still likes me?'

'Obviously. Listen, you don't expect him to be pure, do you?'

'Well, no, but he's a man. And older, too.'

I despaired.

'He doesn't care, or he wouldn't be seeing you,' I said.

'So you don't think I have to tell him about my old boyfriends?'

'God no. Do you want to hear about Ralph's old girlfriends?'

'No!'

'Take my advice, begin your life over, starting with the day you met Ralph.'

TWENTY-SEVEN

I'd barely gotten inside the door when Dellaphine called out to me from the kitchen.

'Mrs Pearlie,' she said, 'a telegram come
for you. It's on the hall table.'

Telegrams were rarely good news these
days, so I ripped open the Western Union
envelope with trembling hands, then heaved
a sigh of relief. Orazio Rossi invited me to
dinner. Tonight. With apologies for the short
notice, he asked me to meet him at seven
p.m. in the Presidential Restaurant of the
Mayflower Hotel.

Accepting Rossi's invitation was out of the
question.

How could I show up at the Mayflower
Hotel yet again, and with a man who worked
for the Onetos? If anyone I knew saw me –
like Joan, for example – and it got back to
OSS, well, I didn't want to think about the
consequences.

How likely was that, though? Not very; the
Presidential Restaurant was expensive. Besides, wouldn't it seem odd if I didn't
accept? That's what I could tell Melinsky. He
didn't have a high regard for me, anyway.

This might be my last chance to talk to someone in the Oneto inner circle about Alessa. Rossi's role had intrigued me ever since I'd heard that Lucia had given him a diamond bracelet right off her wrist. And why had he invited me in the first place? Perhaps he wanted to talk about Alessa's death himself. If so, I'd be all ears.

I called Western Union and sent a telegram to Rossi accepting his invitation.

'Dellaphine,' I called out as I went upstairs, 'I won't be here for dinner.'

'Yes, ma'am,' she answered me.

I stood at my closet and considered my wardrobe choices. The Presidential Restaurant was tall cotton, as my grandmother would say. I owned several acceptable dresses, thanks to Ada's reach-me-downs. And I could borrow jewelry from Phoebe. But then a horrible thought struck me. God, this wasn't a romantic invitation, was it? What if Orazio Rossi had seduction on his mind! I wasn't bad looking for a thirty-year-old woman with glasses. I was a widow, and in many men's eyes that meant I was sexually available.

In that case I should dress down. I'd wear my new green suit dress and low heels, enough make-up to be presentable, and a little jewelry, my good watch and my pearls. That should deliver my message loud and clear.

J. Edgar Hoover ate lunch at the Presidential Restaurant in the Mayflower every day: him and lots of other Washington big shots and celebrities. As I waited to be seated, I scanned the restaurant. I didn't see anybody famous, but the room held four hundred tables! Plenty of space on those walls to hang all the state seals and portraits of the first four presidents.

The maître d'hôtel showed me to Rossi's table. He stood up immediately and grasped my hand.

'Thank you for coming,' he said. 'Such a last-minute invitation. So inconsiderate of me.'

'I was happy to accept,' I said. 'My Tuesday evenings are often open.'

Rossi pulled out my chair to seat me. Right away I noticed the table tent, a folded card illustrated with a caricature of Hitler drawn with enormous ears. *Keep talking*, the caption read. *I'm listening.*

'Most of my evenings are open also,' Rossi answered, smiling with me.

Thank God he wasn't wearing black tie. I hadn't thought about that possibility until I was in the taxi on the way here. I wanted to dress down, not look like a rube.

Rossi, his black hair slicked back as always, wore a glen plaid suit that looked British and tailor made. A gold clip secured his tie to his shirt. Well, the Onetos had lived in London for a few months, hadn't they? I guessed that London tailors were less expensive during wartime.

Our liveried waiter appeared at our table ready with a pad and silver pen to take our order.

'A cocktail?' Rossi asked me. 'Please, whatever you want.'

'A Martini,' I said. 'With a splash of vermouth. No olives.'

'I'll have a Calvert and ginger,' Rossi said. 'Do you like oysters?' he asked me.

'Love them, as long as they're not raw or fried.'

'Oysters Casino to start,' Rossi directed the waiter. 'Thank you again for coming,' he said to me. 'I don't have many friends here, and the atmosphere in the apartment is so terribly sad. I needed to get away.'

'How is the Count?'

'Melancholy. He won't talk about books or politics; he listens to classical music and broods. Lina still cries at least once a day. Lucia stays in her room or goes out with friends.'

Our drinks arrived. My Martini was delicious. The Mayflower used a better quality gin than Gordon's.

Rossi had opened the door by speaking of the Onetos first, so he must not mind gossiping about them.

'Tell me, Orazio, do you think Alessa killed herself?' I asked.

Ice tinkled as Rossi fiddled with his high-ball glass. 'I would have said no, except what else could have happened? She was alone in the apartment. We were all out. The police said it was suicide.'

'You told me at the reception that Alessa was quiet on the way home from New York on the train?'

'More than quiet. Somber. Preoccupied. If Sebastian and I had guessed her mood, we would never have gone to Count Sforza's lecture. Of course, if Lucia had not been out too, perhaps murder would be likely!'

'What?' My hand jerked, and a few drops of my Martini sloshed over the rim of my glass.

'Oh, my dear,' Rossi said, reaching across the table and squeezing my hand. 'I wasn't serious! I am sorry I shocked you. It's just that Lucia despised Alessa; I'm sure she's not sorry she's dead.'

Our oysters arrived, and we concentrated on eating them as neatly as possible with the aid of linen napkins the size of small table-cloths. Crisp bits of bacon sprinkled over the oysters complemented their texture perfect-ly.

When we were finished Rossi beckoned to the waiter. 'Shall we switch to champagne?' he asked me.

'Wonderful,' I said.

'And what shall we have to eat?'

We both studied the menu. I couldn't help but linger over the beef selections. I ate it rarely now, and I recollected the haunches on ice in the hotel kitchen. It wasn't the most expensive item on the menu – the lobster thermidor was. But it would be more polite to order chicken or ham.

'We must have beef,' Orazio said. 'I've had none for a week. You?'

'Beef would be delicious. But it's so expensive, Orazio!'

'I've had nothing to spend my salary on for weeks,' he said. 'Let me enjoy it.'

Rossi ordered us porterhouse steaks with peas, creamed mushrooms, and Potatoes Anna.

When the champagne came, Orazio raised his flute. 'Let's toast to fun and friends,' he said, 'despite the war.'

'I agree,' I said and sipped from my glass. I adored champagne: one of the many tastes I'd acquired over the past year that would set all four of my grandparents spinning in their graves.

'So,' I said, 'you said Lucia disliked Alessa. I don't understand why. She was a lovely person.'

'She was,' Orazio said. 'But, you see, Lucia wanted a daughter-in-law she could dominate. That was never Alessa. And Lucia blamed Alessa for encouraging Sebastian's frugality. Lucia loves to spend money.'

And give away diamond bracelets, I remembered.

'When Lucia plays cards and loses, I pawn jewelry for her,' Orazio said, as if he had read my mind. 'Her debts are piling up. Sebastian has no idea. He can afford to redeem them, but he might refuse, and Alessa would have supported him, even at the risk of losing some family pieces forever. Then there was Alessa's family, respectable minor aristocracy only,' he continued. 'But Alessa's father–' he lowered his voice – 'had an illegitimate son with the daughter of one of the Mafia chieftains in the local village. And insisted on supporting the child. Sebastian married Alessa against Lucia's wishes. They were very happy. But Sebastian is young, and perhaps Lucia hopes he will remarry appropriately.'

The Mafia. Alessa's brother was a Mafia chieftain's grandson. Enzo was Mafia, small potatoes indeed, but *Mafioso* nonetheless. The Mafia ran the unions and the New York City docks. The sleeper who Alessa's asset had been about to reveal to us was Mafia. Could the Mafia reach into a grand hotel in Washington and murder Alessa? No, it was ridiculous. This was the real world, not a Jimmy Cagney movie.

'Louise, you are looking so thoughtful,'

Orazio said. 'You are thinking I shouldn't gossip about my employers so!'

'I'm sorry, not at all!' I said. 'I was thinking about Alessa.'

Pushing his dinner plate to the side, Orazio pulled the champagne bottle out of the silver ice bucket and refilled our flutes. I couldn't finish my steak and asked the waiter for a brown bag when he cleared the table.

'I have little to talk about other than my work and the Onetos,' Rossi said. 'But I am determined to remedy that. If I am to live here for the duration of the war, I need friends. Which leads me to my next request of you.'

Oh no! This was a date after all! Damn! How would I extricate myself from this?

The waiter brought us coffee, pouring it from a gleaming silver pot, reminding me of Enzo toiling in the sub-basement, filthy with silver tarnish.

'There is a USO benefit ball here Friday night. Would you like to go with me? Sebastian and Alessa bought tickets, and Sebastian has given them to me.'

'Well,' I said. A ball. I'd never been to a ball.

'I know it is short notice,' Rossi said. 'But it will be so gay. Gene Kelly and Mary Martin will perform, and many other celebrities are attending. There's a buffet dinner and dancing to the Mayflower Orchestra.'

If I went, I thought, I'd have another chance to learn the geography of the hotel, perhaps talk to some of the staff, and maybe add facts to the timeline of the night Alessa died. Maybe I could even bluff my way into the Oneto apartment again and look for her knitting bag! It would be risky; I wouldn't want to be seen with Rossi by anyone from OSS who knew about Alessa. But how likely was that? Balls at the Mayflower drew thousands of people, and the tickets must be too expensive for most people I knew in OSS.

'Please,' Rossi said. 'I know it's wartime, but can't we enjoy ourselves for one evening?'

I said yes.

It wasn't late when I returned to 'Two Trees'. I insisted on paying for the taxi myself, though Orazio offered. I pleaded work as a reason not to stay for music and dancing, but it was really the early breakfast with policeman Ralph that was on my mind.

'There you are,' Joe said, meeting me in the hall. He quickly kissed me on the cheek as Phoebe called out to me from the lounge.

'Louise, dear,' Phoebe said. 'Come join us.' She and Ada, who didn't work on Tuesday nights, were listening to an Ellery Queen mystery, so I dutifully hung up my coat and went into the lounge trailed by Joe. We would never have a moment's privacy as long as we lived here, I thought desperately.

I wedged myself between Phoebe and Ada on the davenport. Ada wore a new pair of chic lounging pajamas. Phoebe's hair was set in crimps with bobby pins hidden under a towel turban.

Without thinking I placed my brown bag – stamped with The Mayflower Hotel's trademark sailing ship and words 'The Presidential Restaurant' – on the cocktail table.

'Dearie,' Ada said, 'did you go to the Presidential Restaurant tonight?'

'Yes,' I said, furious with myself for being so careless. 'I had dinner with a friend.'

'Who?' Phoebe said. 'Tell us!'

'I hope he paid,' Ada said. 'It's so expensive! Did you see any celebrities? I heard Norman Rockwell is staying there, sketching in the lobby.'

'No,' I said, glancing at Joe.

'You wouldn't see many celebrities on a Tuesday,' Phoebe said. 'They're still recovering from the weekend parties.'

I'd made Joe unhappy. I could tell by the way he didn't meet my eyes and turned away from me. He set about cleaning and refilling his pipe, his usual distraction.

As few lies as possible, please, I reminded myself.

'I had dinner with a friend of Alessa's. We talked about her, that's all.'

'The countess who killed herself?' Phoebe

asked. Hearing her words hurt.

'A man friend? And you wore that dress to the Presidential Restaurant?' Ada asked.

'Yes,' I said. 'It wasn't a date.'

Joe silently tamped down his tobacco and drew on his pipe, sucking in flames from a match to ignite it. I loved the smell of his tobacco.

'It must have been a nice change from Scholl's,' Joe said quietly, referring to the chain restaurant we'd eaten in over the weekend.

That's not fair, damn it, I thought to myself. But then I was the idiot who'd brought home the leftovers from my elegant dinner in a labeled brown bag. I didn't answer Joe. I couldn't tell him I'd rather eat a tuna sandwich on a park bench with him than go to any fancy restaurant in town, not in front of Phoebe and Ada. And I certainly couldn't tell him that I was Pinkerton-ing Alessa's death on my own. What would he think when I told him about the ball!

Oh, what did it matter? Joe and I didn't have a real romance, anyway, and likely never would. We were trapped by lack of money and social convention. After the war he'd go back to Europe and I'd stay here and consider myself fortunate if I had a job and lived in a comfortable boarding house for the rest of my life. And that presumed I wouldn't lose this job! Going to college and having my own apartment one day were dreams, too. Lovely dreams, but not sensible.

'I'm tired,' I said. 'I'm going on to bed. Have to get up early tomorrow.'

'Don't forget to put your leftovers in the refrigerator,' Joe said.

TWENTY-EIGHT

Ralph's daily breakfast cafe was a greasy spoon. If I were on my own I wouldn't set foot in the place. I could hardly see through the plate-glass window on account of the steam and grease coating it.

I spotted Ralph right away at a table for two in a back corner. He waved, and five seconds after I'd sat down the colored waitress poured me a mug of coffee.

'I see a sugar bowl,' I said to him. 'I don't believe it!'

Ralph grinned at me. 'I'm a cop,' he said. 'There's always sugar on the table for me.'

Ralph ordered a stack of pancakes and sausage. I requested bacon and fried eggs over medium.

The waitress warmed up our mugs of coffee before she left.

'I guess cops get all the coffee they want, too?' I said.

'Yes, ma'am!' He smiled. 'One of the rewards of public service.' He reached behind him, where his blue jacket hung over the back of the chair, and pulled a folded sheaf of papers out of a pocket. 'Here,' he said matter-of-factly, 'is the paperwork you wanted.' Just like that.

I took the papers from him and stuffed them into my pocketbook. 'When do you need them back?'

'No hurry. Anyone looking for them will think the file is lost.'

I flinched. I spent my life at OSS making sure files were in their proper slots. Finding information, or not finding it, could save lives, or lose them.

The bacon was crisp, and my eggs were fried the way I liked them, with only a bit of soft center. We even had real jam for our toast! I could see the benefits of befriending a policeman. I hoped Betty had the brains to hang on to him.

Back at 'Two Trees' in my bedroom I spread the contents of the file Ralph had given me across my bed. Despite the rush to judgment on Alessa's case the file was surprisingly thorough. There were no photographs, thank God. These days sleazy crime photographers crawled over any public death, hoping for a picture that would land them on the front page of a big newspaper. They weren't reluctant to mess with the scene to improve the shot, either. I'd dreaded seeing a photograph of Alessa dead.

The skimpy police artist sketch was disturbing enough.

For one thing the artist hadn't bothered with facial features. Alessa's body lay outstretched under covers, her faceless head on a pillow, one hand dangling over the edge of the bed. A liquor bottle and a glass sat on her bedside table. I hadn't noticed them when I'd visited her bedroom the afternoon of her memorial service.

I flipped through the police report. 'Deceased was in the habit of drinking a tumbler of Fernet before bed,' I read. What on earth was Fernet?

The next drawing showed the inside of Lucia Oneto's medicine cabinet, with her bottle of laudanum and Nembutal tablets. 'The decedent's mother-in-law, Lucia Oneto, stated that a substantial amount of laudanum, over two teaspoons, and perhaps several Nembutal tablets were missing from her prescriptions. She also stated that the decedent and she shared the bathroom, and that the decedent knew the medications were in the medicine cabinet. As far as she knew the decedent never took the medications before.'

The standard dose of laudanum was one and a half milliliters – Phoebe used a dropper to dose herself. It tasted awful. 'Perhaps the Fernet,' the report went on, 'made taking the laudanum palatable, and the Nembutal tablets brought on sleep before the uncomfortable side effects of the laudanum occurred.'

Wouldn't it also be possible, I wondered, for a murderer to dose Alessa's tonic with laudanum and Nembutal? Or force her to take them, followed by the Fernet?

As the members of the Oneto household were all foreign nationals, their fingerprints were on file. Lucia's fingerprints were on the medications; Alessa's on the Fernet bottle and tumbler. Of course, fingerprints could be wiped away.

What in heaven's name was Fernet!

I slid off the bed and went downstairs, where I found Phoebe in the lounge with her mending. She was stitching a new ribbon border around the edge of a worn but still serviceable wool blanket.

'Phoebe,' I said, 'do you know what Fernet is?'

'The drink? It's a horrible Italian liqueur. Awful taste. Full of herbs and spices. It's like bitters, only worse. Why do you ask?'

'A friend of mine uses it as a tonic.'

'With all the stuff that's in it it's bound to cure something.'

Once upstairs again I went back to the police report.

Alessa's household had alibis. Sebastian and Orazio attended a lecture together. Lucia was with friends who verified her presence. Lina spent her evening off with friends.

According to Sebastian, when he came home, he found his wife sleeping peacefully in their bed. When he awoke the next morning she was dead beside him.

Both Sebastian and Orazio said that Alessa had seemed somber and sad before they'd gone out that evening.

I understood why the police, the coroner – and the Oneto family, for that matter – thought Alessa had killed herself. The circumstantial evidence was overwhelming.

Discouraged, I turned to the transcribed police interviews.

Alessa's husband and his private secretary had attended Count Sforza's lecture on the future of Italy after Mussolini. Then I clutched at the page and reread the next few words, stunned. Sforza's lecture was at the Mayflower! Sebastian and Orazio were at the hotel all evening!

The lecture was held in the Chinese Room, near the Seventeenth Street entrance, followed by a reception. Some alibis! You'd never convince me that either Sebastian or Orazio couldn't have found an excuse to slip away from the lecture long enough to go back upstairs to the apartment and poison Alessa's tonic.

And Lucia Oneto was literally right across the Seventeenth Street lobby from the Chinese Room, in the Ladies Parlor! I had assumed she'd be playing bridge in a friend's apartment. She could easily have excused herself go to the ladies' room or down the promenade for a sherry while she was the 'dummy'!

When I'd first learned that Sebastian, Orazio, and Lucia were 'out' when Alessa died, I'd assumed they were off the hotel premises. Instead they were in the May-flower all along, an elevator ride away from the Oneto apartment!

Lina was the only person who had what I considered a good alibi. She'd been at the movies with two friends. They'd gone out for milkshakes afterwards.

I reminded myself the murderer didn't have to be Orazio, Sebastian, or Lucia. The Mayflower was the grandest hotel in Washington, crammed with hundreds of people at all hours. Anyone could have entered the hotel from one of its four entrances, taken the elevator to the fifth floor, knocked on the Onetos' apartment door and been admitted. Including Enzo, the Mafia soldier. The possibilities made me want to tear at my hair!

And, of course, while they were conducting the investigation, the DC Police had no idea that Alessa was a floater for the OSS, and that her 'operation' to deliver the name of a sleeper agent had ended with her death.

How could I possibly sort all this out by

going to a benefit ball? It was hopeless. But I was going to try anyway.

I had no choice.

TWENTY-NINE

I needed a ball gown, but I quailed at the thought of what it might cost. I'd heard from Ada it was possible to open a charge account at some department stores and pay for purchases over time. I sure hoped so. I checked my watch. I'd have a sandwich and go shopping straight away.

Downstairs I found Phoebe still hemming the new ribbon border on to her frayed blanket. I sat down next to her and tried to figure out what I needed to say.

'Spit it out, dearie,' she said.

'I have to go to a ball,' I said. 'The USO benefit ball at the Mayflower on Friday night. I'm off to find a dress.'

'Let me guess,' she said, 'you don't want to tell Joe.'

I felt sick. 'Let's put it this way,' I said. 'I need to tell him myself.'

Phoebe lost the thread from her needle. After watching her fail to re-thread it twice, I took it from her.

'Let me do that,' I said. After threading the needle, I handed it back to her.

'Thank you,' she said.

'You should get glasses.' I pushed my own up the bridge of my nose.

'I know. Dellaphine pesters me about it all the time. And most of my friends have spectacles. When I was a young woman no self-respecting debutante or young matron wore glasses.'

'I don't care; I'd rather see.'

'So,' Phoebe said. 'You said "had to" go to the ball at the Mayflower. Does that mean you don't want to go?'

'Not at all.'

'So why are you going?'

Desperately, I fell back on the standard wartime excuse. 'I can't say right now,' I said.

'I understand. Are you going to Woodies for your gown?'

'Do you know somewhere cheaper? Maybe a consignment shop?'

'Dearie,' she said, 'this is a big bash at one of the grandest hotels in the world left standing. You must make your best effort. You're an attractive young woman with lovely manners and a brain. Make the most of it!'

'That's so kind of you.'

'You're as good as any woman who will be there. Your dress should be as fine as you can afford. So many career women ignore their looks, and it's such a mistake.'

She was right, of course. Times hadn't

changed enough for me to go to a fancy event poorly dressed and expect to be taken seriously.

Without thinking I'd worn my Sears catalog man-styled trousers and a dull-gray button-ed up cardigan to shop for my gown. The minute I walked into the women's evening wear department at Woodies I felt like a country bumpkin.

Warm ivory walls reflected soft lighting from crystal lamps. Pink roses and chrysan-themums in silvered glass vases were scatter-ed tastefully on occasional tables. A few wing-back chairs, upholstered in ivory silk brocade – before the war, of course – sat in front of a sort of raised platform, a stage, really, near the dressing rooms, where rich husbands could pass judgment on their wives' selections.

The room was lined with racks of jewel-toned or jet black cocktail dresses and ball gowns. Light reflected off yards of sequins and satin. Tulle, lace, and crêpe crinolines and overskirts poked out from the racks into the showroom.

'What department are you looking for, dear?' a saleswoman asked.

'Here,' I said. 'I mean, this one.'

She eyed me critically from head to foot. 'Are you sure?' she asked. The saleswoman, whose name tag identified her as Marian, was dressed perfectly for her role. She wore a beautifully tailored shirtwaist dress in expensive wool with a double strand of pearls and pearl earrings.

'Yes,' I said, determined, remembering Phoebe's words.

'Well,' she said, 'let's get started. What function are you attending?'

'The USO benefit ball at the Mayflower Hotel Friday night,' I said.

'*This* Friday night!'

'Yes,' I said.

'No time for alterations, then,' she said. 'The dress will need to fit perfectly.'

'I can hem it myself.'

Her surprised look that told me that her customers didn't hem dresses.

'What size do you wear?'

'Ten.'

'All right, let's see what we can find.' She led me over to a nearby rack. 'You'll want black, of course, so you can wear it again. How about this one?'

She pulled out a stunning black gown with cap sleeves and elegant ivory lace insets in the bodice. The dress seemed to drop like a waterfall from neckline to hem. My heart stopped. I loved it.

'Would you like to try it on?'

I didn't want to disappoint myself by trying on this dress if I couldn't afford it.

'How much is it?' I asked.

'My dear,' she said, 'it's an Adrian. It's one hundred and seventy eight dollars.'

My instincts were correct. 'I can't possibly afford that.'

'Oh,' she said, disappointed, her commission dwindling before her eyes. 'Well, let's go over to this rack. These are all Woodward and Lothrop house brands, you understand, but they are designed by some promising couturiers. All under a hundred dollars.'

'That's fine,' I said. It wasn't fine, but I could manage it.

'Here,' she said, riffling through the rack. 'Two very nice black...'

A bit of blueberry flashed by in the clutch of dresses Marian shoved over the rod as she searched for black gowns.

'I want to try on that one,' I said, pointing at the blue dress.

Marian pulled the blueberry frock out and hung it on a display hook.

It was adorable. It wasn't silk, but everyone wore rayon these days. Its heart shaped, fitted bodice was appliquéd with ivory flowers inside the pleated bust. Tiny self-fabric buttons trimmed the front. The waist was pleated, and the bias-cut skirt, lined with blue acetate, fell in the fullest sweep permitted by the War Production Board. Thin spaghetti straps finished the look.

'My dear,' Marian said, 'don't you think this is a bit revealing about the neck and shoulders for a woman your age?'

'Where is the dressing room?' I asked.

The gown fit me like it had been made for me. Back outside in the showroom I admired myself in front of a full-length mirror in the flattering soft light. The dress didn't even need hemming.

'I was wrong,' Marian said. 'You look lovely. You have kept up your figure nicely.'

It was almost worth losing my job to be able to wear this gown. To a ball at the Mayflower, no less! If only I was going with Joe, and not Orazio Rossi.

'Can you see without your glasses?'

'Not a thing.'

'That's too bad,' she said. At least she didn't suggest that I remove them and stumble about blindly for the sake of beauty.

Best of all, I could accessorize this dress with black. I owned respectable black evening slippers, and I knew I could borrow gloves, an evening cape, and a handbag from either Ada or Phoebe.

'How much is it?' I asked.

'Seventy-nine dollars.'

If I couldn't buy it on time it would take every cent I had.

At the cash register I summoned up my nerve. 'I'd like to open a charge account,' I said.

'Are you a government girl?' Marian asked.

'Yes.'

'Did you bring a pay stub with you?'

'Yes,' I said, relieved.

'I'll write it up. One third is due now, and then two more payments over two months. The store will send you notices when the payments are due.'

I emptied my wallet. Marian hung my new ball gown on a pink silk padded hanger and carefully protected it with a Woodward and Lothrop dress bag. Cinderella, that was me!

I slipped inside the house, intending to sneak upstairs with my garment bag. So far Phoebe was the only person at home who knew I was going to a Mayflower ball, and I wasn't ready to announce it yet.

Instead I ran right into Joe, who came out of the lounge.

'I thought I recognized your footstep,' he said, warmth in his brown eyes. Then he saw the long Woodies garment bag draped over my arm.

My heart sank.

'Been shopping?' he asked.

'Yes,' I said. 'It's a ball gown.'

'Going somewhere special?'

'I've been meaning to tell you...'

'I'm sure you have.'

'It's not a date! I'm going to a benefit ball at the Mayflower Hotel Friday night,' I said, the words tumbling out of me, getting it over with as soon as possible.

'Wow,' he said. 'That's – what is that expression you use? – tall cotton.' When Joe's mouth tightened like that, there seemed to be no break between his moustache and beard, giving him an uncharacteristically fierce aspect.

'It's not a date,' I said again. 'I'm going with a friend. He had an extra ticket.' I could hardly tell Joe the truth.

'Best hang your dress up, or it will get wrinkled before the big night,' Joe said. He wasn't often sarcastic, but when he was he seemed like a different person than the man I'd known for almost a year. I didn't like it.

'I will,' I said.

I went up the staircase, and Joe went back in the lounge, pulling his pipe out of his jacket pocket as he went.

THIRTY

'Look what I found,' Phoebe said, brandishing a liqueur bottle. It was almost dinner time, and Joe, Ada, and I had gathered in the lounge to listen to the news. Henry hadn't arrived home yet.

'What?' I asked.

'Fernet!' Phoebe said. 'I thought I had a bottle somewhere. It was a gift from someone ages ago.'

'What's Fernet?' Ada asked.

'An Italian liqueur. Made from herbs and spices. Louise was asking about it,' she said.

Joe turned down the radio. 'I'm familiar with Fernet,' he said. 'In Europe it's drunk as a tonic, for health.'

'Let's try some,' Phoebe said.

'I'll get the glasses,' Ada said. She left the lounge and came back from the dining room with four sherry glasses and a corkscrew. Joe deftly extracted the cork and filled our glasses with the caramel-colored cordial. It looked like prune juice.

I was eager to taste it. I wanted to know if it would disguise the harsh taste of enough laudanum to kill a person.

I sipped from my glass and almost gagged on its bitter taste, like a mixture of black licorice and mouthwash. Its pungent aroma filled my nostrils, found its way to my lungs, and made me gasp.

'God,' Ada said, 'it's revolting.'

'It must be good for you, because no one would drink this for its taste,' Joe said. He held up the bottle and read out the ingredients. 'Mushrooms, fermented beets, coco leaf, gentian, wormwood ... and the list goes on. Not to mention the forty-five percent alcohol content.'

I had my answer. Alessa could have downed this liqueur doctored with a couple of teaspoons of laudanum and a ground-up Nembutal tablet with no knowledge she was being poisoned. So she *could* have been murdered! Instead of feeling upset, as I expected, I was relieved to have the question resolved.

Phoebe made a face, and we all set our glasses down on the table.

'So much for that,' Phoebe said. 'Let's have some sherry instead, shall we? After all, tomorrow is a holiday.'

'I'll get fresh glasses,' I said.

'I'll find the sherry and pour this down the kitchen sink, if it's OK with you, Phoebe,' Joe said, gesturing with the Fernet bottle.

'Please do,' Phoebe said. 'And would you

two see that Dellaphine and Madeleine get a glass of sherry also, before you come back?'

As I collected fresh sherry glasses in the dining room and arranged them on a tray – six this time, since Henry still wasn't home – Joe came in from the kitchen to pour the sherry.

He put a hand on mine. 'I'm sorry,' he said.

'It's me who should be sorry,' I said. 'I handled this badly. I can't explain the real reason why I have to go to this shindig, but I swear it's not a date.'

'I believe you,' Joe said, 'because I can't bear not to.'

'I never thought I'd see the day when I'd use canned food to fix Thanksgiving dinner,' Dellaphine said.

'It's just pumpkin for the pies,' Phoebe said.

'It's the principle of the thing,' Dellaphine answered.

My dinner-roll dough finished its first rising. I dusted my hands with flour and turned the dough out on to a floury wooden board, kneading it with the heels of both hands. The yeasty odor reminded me that I liked baking, though I rarely did any these days.

'Dellaphine, do you think this is ready?' I asked.

Dellaphine dried her hands and fingered the dough. 'Yes, ma'am, it's ready,' she said.

'Can I make cloverleaf rolls?' I asked.

'Sure,' she said. 'The pan is in the right lower side of the Hoosier cabinet.'

I found two muffin pans, black with age, and greased them with a butter wrapper we'd been hoarding. Dellaphine allowed me a little melted butter to dip the tiny balls I formed of the dough into before I put three of them in each muffin compartment. I covered both pans with towels and found a warm spot on top of the stove to allow them to rise for the second time.

'What time will we eat?' I asked. 'Ada's playing for the midday Thanksgiving meal at the Willard Hotel. She said she thought she'd be home by two.'

'Henry said his boss told him he could leave at three,' Phoebe said. 'Will Madeleine get out early today?' she asked Dellaphine.

'Yes, ma'am, but she don't know what time,' Dellaphine said.

'Let's plan for dinner at four,' Phoebe said. 'If necessary we'll wait for Madeleine.' Dellaphine and Madeleine might eat in the kitchen, but Phoebe wouldn't sit down to Thanksgiving dinner until Dellaphine's daughter was home.

Joe stood in the kitchen door. 'Can I help?' he asked, looking stoic.

'Yes, indeed,' Dellaphine said. 'You can go

outside and shuck them oysters.'

Joe appeared disconcerted. 'I know oysters,' he said, 'but "shuck" is a new word for me.'

'I'll show you how it's done,' I said. I'd shucked oysters at my parents' fish camp for years. 'You'll need to wear gloves.'

On the back porch, bundled up in coats and scarves, Joe and I perched on the brick steps with a basket of oysters and a mixing bowl between us. A few autumn leaves still clung to the trees. Joe and Henry had burned all the fallen leaves last weekend, and a ring of charred grass showed where the pile had blazed in the center of the remains of our Victory Garden. Earlier I'd turned the soil over after fertilizing it with the pile of vegetable scraps I'd composted, ready for next year's planting.

Our Victory chickens, as Ada called them, huddled in their house, feathers ruffled against the cold. They laid fewer eggs in cold weather. Phoebe had needed to purchase a dozen at the market for the Thanksgiving baking.

'This,' I said to Joe, 'is a shucker.' I handed him the flat two-sided pointed blade. It was about four inches long with a short handle and guard to protect your hand. 'Hold the oyster like this, along the hinge. Be careful: the shell is sharp, and so is the shucker.' I demonstrated how to shove the point of the shucker between the lips of the oyster, twist it, and force the reluctant oyster shell open. 'You want to separate the meat from this thick muscle here and dump the oyster and liquor into the bowl.'

'This is harder than it looks,' Joe said, struggling with the knobbly, slippery shell.

'Like anything, it takes practice.'

Soon Joe was shucking like an expert, and before long we had about a pint of oysters to show for our labors.

'We'll mix these into the stuffing,' I said. 'Let's go dump the shells into the chicken pen.'

'What on earth for?' he asked.

'Calcium. Makes the eggshells strong.'

Down at the chicken pen we flung the oyster shells over the fence and watched the chickens fight over the bits of muscle and meat that still clung to them.

'I didn't know chickens were such scavengers,' he said.

This surprised me. Joe often told me how he visited his grandparents' farm outside Prague every summer. Surely, he'd seen chickens fed scraps before.

'They're like pigs,' I said. 'They'll eat anything.'

'Are we out of sight?' Joe asked, angling his head back to look at the house.

'Of course not,' I said.

So he didn't kiss me, but took my arm and

put it through his, and we lingered outside, enjoying each other's warmth and company.

Joe broke the comfortable silence first. 'Did you see the paper this morning?' he asked.

'No. Why?'

He squeezed my arm. 'It appears the Nazi siege of Malta has ended. A convoy passed through the island from Alexandria intact on the twentieth of November.'

'No bombers?'

'Not one.'

Relief washed through my body. Rachel and her children were truly safe now.

'That is wonderful news,' I said. 'Wonderful.'

'Add it to the success of Torch and the Russian victory at Stalingrad, and it seems we have a chance to win this war.'

'You had doubts?'

'Yes, the Allies got such a late start. Almost too late.'

Dellaphine called to us from the kitchen door, asking for her oysters.

When we got back into the kitchen, Dellaphine watched us break up a pan of cornbread and mix the oysters into it. She added some bacon fat, onions, sage, and a liberal shake of Durkee Poultry Seasoning. We stuffed the turkey and had enough left to fill an extra pan to eat with leftovers.

Dellaphine and I covered the turkey breast

with slices of thick maple-cured bacon. Joe lifted the heavy turkey in its roasting pan and slid it into the oven.

Dellaphine wiped perspiration from her face with a bright pink bandanna she'd stuck in her apron pocket. It was hot in the kitchen and would get hotter as the day progressed.

'I think I can rest a spell now,' Dellaphine said, stretching, massaging her back with her big hands. 'The cranberry sauce and potatoes are cooking, and the squash and onions are chopped and ready to fry when the turkey comes out of the oven.'

'Everything smells delicious,' Joe said.

'Have you eaten Thanksgiving dinner before?' I asked.

'I was in the country this time last year, but this is my first Thanksgiving dinner. I was living in a cold-water walk up in Baltimore and didn't know a soul well enough to ask me to a meal.'

'Wait until the turkey starts to roast,' I said. 'The aroma is like nothing else.'

'By the way, where's Phoebe?' Joe asked.

Dellaphine plopped on to a kitchen chair and fanned herself with her bandanna. 'She went upstairs to put her feet up, she said,' Dellaphine answered.

We knew what that meant. That was Phoebe's code for dosing herself with laudanum for one of her sick headaches.

'She'll be missing her boys,' Dellaphine

said defensively, noticing our expressions. 'It being a holiday and all.'

'I hope she's careful,' Joe said. 'That stuff is dangerous.'

'She is,' Dellaphine said. 'Besides, I keep my eye on that bottle. And on the sleeping pills, too.'

The warm kitchen, the good news about Malta, the contented feeling of standing arm and arm with Joe all receded, as sharply as an airplane disappearing over the horizon.

Alessa was dead of a laudanum overdose, and everyone, even her husband, believed she'd committed suicide. Since tasting the Fernet yesterday, I knew she could have been murdered. The liqueur's bitterness would have disguised the nasty taste of the amount of laudanum and Nembutal necessary to do the job.

'Are you all right?' Joe asked me. Both he and Dellaphine stared at me with concern.

'What do you mean?' I asked.

'I spoke to you, and you didn't answer,' he said. 'You were looking off into the distance.'

'I'm sorry, I was thinking about Malta,' I fibbed.

'Come into the lounge and sit with me,' Joe said. 'We can listen to the President's address from Warm Springs.'

I forced thoughts of Alessa to the back of my mind.

270

Later Phoebe drifted into the room to join us, her pupils almost completely dilated.

'I'm not good for much of anything except laying the table,' Ada said.

'It looks lovely, dear,' Phoebe said. For the first time since I'd come to 'Two Trees' we were using Phoebe's good china, silver and crystal.

'I got these as wedding presents,' Phoebe said. 'It seems so old-fashioned now.' Like Phoebe herself, who, though only nearing fifty, seemed older because she wore her skirts several inches below her knee and crimped her hair.

'I think it's all beautiful,' I said, from the perspective of a bride who'd gotten no wedding gifts. I'd married Bill in the midst of the Depression. If his job as a telegrapher hadn't included the small apartment above the Wilmington Western Union building, we couldn't have married at all.

We heard Madeleine come in the back door from work, and Phoebe left us to go into the kitchen.

'Did you hear about Malta?' I asked Ada. 'And Stalingrad? And El Alamein?'

'That's all everyone talked about at the Willard.' She lowered her voice. 'It's awful of me, isn't it, to hope that Rein is dead.' Rein was Ada's husband, the German pilot who'd left her to join the Nazis and the Luftwaffe.

'I don't think it's awful. I wish lots of people dead, starting at the top.' Hitler himself. Why was it that someone hadn't assassinated the man yet? I couldn't understand it.

We heard the front door slam. It was Henry arriving home.

'Henry's here,' Joe said, coming in from the lounge. 'Does this mean we can eat? I'm actually slavering.'

We crowded into the kitchen to admire the turkey as it came out of the oven. To our surprise Henry brought a contribution to the meal. He sheepishly handed two bottles of champagne over to Phoebe.

'It's already chilled,' Henry said. 'The wine shop near the bus stop was open until four.'

'Thank you, Henry, how wonderful!' Phoebe said. 'Ada and Louise, can you find the champagne flutes? The rest of you get out of here so Dellaphine and I can dish this up.'

Henry carved the turkey on the sideboard while Joe poured champagne into Phoebe's crystal flutes. Ada and I washed them first, as they were so dusty with disuse.

We loaded our plates with turkey, oyster stuffing, cranberry sauce, mashed potatoes, baked winter squash, creamed onions, and hot cloverleaf rolls, then picked up our champagne and went to the table. Dellaphine and Madeleine followed us, filling their plates and taking a flute each. They stayed long enough to join us in prayer before carrying their meals into the kitchen.

Phoebe's prayer was the standard Episcopalian grace, which seemed way too Anglican Prayer Book and short to suit my Southern Baptist upbringing, but it did cover all the bases. 'Bless O Lord this food to our use, and us to your loving service, and keep us ever mindful of the needs of others, we ask in Christ's name, amen!'

'Amen!' we chorused, and for the next couple of hours we put our troubles aside and were thankful for all that was good in the world.

THIRTY-ONE

Later that evening when I was alone upstairs in my bedroom, sitting cross-legged on my bed with my notebook open, I put Thanksgiving behind me and focused on the mess I was in.

For the last week I'd snooped around Alessa's death like the amateur I was, poking into police and OSS files without authority and openly quizzing everyone I could locate who knew Alessa. I'd implied that she was murdered without thinking of what that meant. Now that I knew she could have dosed herself with laudanum and Nembutal without realizing it, I recognized the grave danger I was in. Her killer would be happy to dispatch me, too.

What did I hope to accomplish by going to this ball with Orazio tomorrow night? I could scout the scene. Where was the nearest bank of elevators to the Chinese Room, where Sebastian and Orazio had attended Count Sforza's lecture, and to the Ladies Parlor, where Lucia had played bridge? I remembered how huge the Mayflower was.

The rooms where Sebastian, Orazio, and Lucia spent the evening of Alessa's death were almost a full block away from the hotel's main entrance. How long would it take to get from those rooms to the Onetos' apartment? How long did the bridge break last? The Sforza lecture intermission? The lecture reception? The hotel would be jammed packed with people who'd been there that night who might be able to answer my questions.

If Alessa had been murdered, which seemed more and more likely to me, was it personal or related to her mission?

If it was personal, Lucia, Sebastian, or Rossi must be her murderer. She didn't know anyone else. What motives could the three of them have? Either Sebastian adored his wife and was grief-stricken, or he was a better actor than Olivier. He had no motive that I could see. And Rossi? Why would he want her dead? Lucia, though, was a possibility. She hated Alessa for being independent, for postponing children, and for endorsing Sebastian's frugality.

Or if Alessa's murder had been due to her mission, who were the suspects? The Mafia sleeper whose name Alessa had brought back from New York to turn over to OSS? How did I know Enzo didn't work for him, that his story was true? Besides, if Enzo was *Mafioso*, the Mayflower likely harbored more

Mafia small fish eager to make their bosses happy.

Who could help me? Only Orazio, it seemed.

I would have to handle all this delicately to avoid suspicion. And I was an amateur. A file clerk who'd fallen into an operation. Three days at 'The Farm' hardly prepared me to pull this off.

Speaking of suspicion, I was attending this very public ball with Orazio Rossi following being suspended for insubordination after attending a reception at the Onetos' apartment. Any number of well-heeled OSS people who knew me could be there. Joan Adams, for example. She ran with a wealthy crowd. Don Murray, my boss, whose mother was a Peoples Drug Store heir. Bill Donovan himself, if he was back from Europe.

If I was seen by the wrong people with Rossi, flouting my instructions to stay away from the Onetos, I could kiss my career goodbye. It might not be the best career in the world, annotating and filing index cards and files, but it was the only one I had.

My second goal, of course, was to go through Alessa's knitting bag looking for the information I wanted. How could I possibly get into the apartment to search? Maybe by the end of the evening I could trust Rossi enough to enlist his help.

I could avoid all this. I could call Orazio

and tell him I had sprained my ankle, or was down with the flu. I didn't have to go and risk everything.

But Alessa had risked everything ... and lost. How could I do less?

Scared and sleepless, I padded down the hall to Phoebe's room to ask for a Nembutal so I could get some rest.

THIRTY-TWO

'You don't need to stand out here with me,' I said. 'I'm perfectly able to wait for a taxi by myself.'

'A gentleman doesn't let a beautiful woman stand on a curb alone,' Joe said.

I did look nice. My blueberry-colored dress was even prettier on me in natural light than it was in the Woodies Dress Salon. Phoebe had lent me a black lace evening shawl and black kid evening gloves that fastened above my elbow with a pearl button. The rhinestone and zircon lavaliere and earrings she'd given me last summer looked perfect. And Ada had found a black beaded bag large enough to hold my compact, lipstick, money, house key, and my knife. My knife, what a joke!

I'd be excited about this evening, especially now that Joe was OK with it, if I wasn't terrified of being seen by someone from OSS. Or confirming that Alessa was murdered.

Where was my taxi? The cold air crept under my shawl.

'You're jiggling,' Joe said, his voice muffled by the scarf wrapped around his face.

'I want the taxi to hurry up and get here,' I said.

'This does have something to do with your job, doesn't it?' Joe asked.

'You know I can't say.'

'Sometimes I think I have a crush on Mata Hari,' he teased.

'It will never amount to more than a crush if we can't find some time to be alone together.'

'I know,' he said.

I wondered if Joan would be willing to lend me her apartment when she visited friends out of town. She might be terribly shocked, but then again I'd been married, so maybe it wouldn't seem too dreadful. Or perhaps Joe could rent one of the many cabins – 'camps', they were called – on the Potomac for a weekend.

My taxi arrived. Joe handed me into it expertly, even lifting my gown so it didn't drag in the dirt as I climbed in, tucking the skirt around me once I was seated. He'd done this before, clearly! I wondered for whom, exactly, and added that to my long list of things I'd like to know about him.

Six blocks away from home my taxi joined a queue of mostly limousines unloading passengers who were dressed to the nines, either in evening wear or dress uniforms. My pulse quickened as the liveried Mayflower hotel footman opened my door and handed me out of my cab. I felt like a movie star attending a Hollywood premiere!

Orazio waited for me at the entrance to the hotel. He took my arm and threaded it through his.

'You look lovely,' he said.

'Thank you. You look nice, too,' I answered.

Orazio wore an impeccably tailored double-breasted tuxedo with satin lapels and a satin stripe down his trousers. His hair was slicked down with brilliantine, as always.

As we moved toward the open doors of the Mayflower and heard the music and throngs of people my excitement mounted. I felt guilty for enjoying myself. I was here because of Alessa – I didn't want to forget that.

The lobby was lit by four priceless bronze and gold torchieres, blazing with gas flames, assisted by massive crystal chandeliers. Red, white, and blue bunting draped the mezzanine rail. A USO banner hung over the front desk. Pretty girls in khaki dresses with USO patches mingled with soldiers and sailors who must have been given tickets. No way they could afford it themselves.

I checked my evening shawl at the cloakroom. The attendant hung it between a full-length mink and an Army nurse's blue cloak.

'We need to walk all the way to the end of the Promenade and back to get the full effect,' Orazio said when I rejoined him.

Twenty-six feet wide and a full block long, from Connecticut Avenue to Seventeenth Street, the Mayflower Promenade was a wide hall through the main floor of the hotel. Along its length it showcased priceless art and antiques. As we strolled, along with hundreds of other guests, we stopped to admire the exhibits.

'I walk through this gallery every day,' Orazio said, 'but at night, when the hotel is lit and decorated for a fancy event, it looks like a palace.'

We gawked at two Louis XIV gold consoles, a collection of Aubusson tapestries, and, of course, the stunning white marble statues that occupied the place of honor in the center of the Promenade: 'The Lost Pleiad' – her hand shading her eyes, searching – 'La Sirene', and 'Flora'.

We passed the Presidential Restaurant, where Orazio and I had dined the other night, on our left and the Mayflower Lounge on our right.

'The bar's set up in here,' Orazio said, steering me into the Lounge. 'I have four drink tickets, but, of course, we can purchase more later.'

'Two drinks is more than enough for me,' I said.

'Would you like a cocktail, or champagne?' he asked.

'Champagne, please.'

He handed me a bubbling flute and took one for himself. I felt so Greta Garbo holding a champagne glass in my gloved hand.

'Let's stop at the ballroom before we go on,' Orazio said. 'We'll come back to the Promenade later.'

We stood inside the door, drinking in the scene. The Ballroom was the most elegant room I'd ever seen. Bunting hung everywhere, obscuring much of the vermilion, gold, and ivory decorative painting. Its high vaulted ceiling was lined on three sides with two tiers of VIP balcony boxes. Black and gold marble pillars separated the boxes. Lush gilt ornamentation crowded what empty space there was between boxes and pillars. Four chandeliers, larger than their fellows in the lobby, lit the room brilliantly.

'That's the presidential box,' Orazio said, pointing, 'where the president sits during Inaugural Balls. And the murals are by one of my countrymen, Ampelio Tonillo, a Venetian.'

Couples already crowded the ballroom, mingling and chatting, waiting for the dance music to begin.

'There's a disappearing stage: it will rise when the music starts. There's a movie screen, too,' Orazio said, 'though they won't be using it tonight.'

'It's a fairy tale,' I said. And I'm Cinderella, I thought.

Orazio squeezed my arm. 'I'm so glad you agreed to come,' he said. 'It would be a shame to waste this.'

'I'm glad, too,' I said, and I was, except that I'd rather I was with Joe.

We turned and continued our stroll down the Promenade.

'Where is Sebastian tonight?' I asked.

'At a friend's apartment for dinner. He couldn't bear to be here. Alessa bought her ball gown at Saks when she was in New York. She brought it back on the train. It's still hanging in her closet. Sebastian has not yet cleaned out any of her things.'

'Poor man.' Would a woman about to kill herself buy an evening gown? I didn't think so.

Orazio bent over to whisper in my ear. 'Sebastian feels a bit guilty, I think,' he said.

'What do you mean?'

'Sebastian loved Alessa wildly – as a man should love his wife, of course. He worried that she was bored here. In fact, she went to New York to see her friends often enough that he fantasized that she had a lover.'

'No!' I said.

'Yes,' he answered. 'When I rode the train with her to New York, he asked me to see if a man met the train. Of course, no one did.

283

It was a ludicrous idea. Now Sebastian feels guilty that he even suspected her.'

'Poor man,' I said.

'Lucia will be here tonight though. Nothing would cause her to miss the opportunity to wear her jewels.'

Except for the diamond bracelet she gave you, I remembered. He'd told me he pawned jewelry for Lucia, but maybe he was a gigolo! I studied him while he waved at an acquaintance across the room. I didn't know any gigolos, but Orazio was handsome and gracious enough to fit the bill.

'Isn't the Chinese Room at this end of the Promenade?' I asked.

'Yes,' Orazio said. 'Sebastian and I were at a lecture there the night Alessa died. Would you like to see it? It's as stunning as the Ballroom in its own way.'

'Yes, please, I've heard so much about it.'

Orazio pushed open a door and led me into a salon glowing with the reds and blues of the Chinese Chippendale style. The walls gleamed with gilt and red lacquer murals. Although smaller than any of the other rooms we'd seen, it still seemed huge by my standards.

'How many people were at the Count's lecture?' I asked.

'Oh, a couple hundred or so. Count Sforza is a fine speaker and a good man. If it were not for him, America would think all Italians were either fascists or mobsters.'

'That's not so!' I said.

'You don't think so? I'm glad to hear it. But Sforza is an aristocrat. When the war is finally won, and Mussolini is dead, the people of Italy, and Sicily, will reject the monarchy and govern themselves. For the first time in its history, Italy's wealth will be distributed to everyone.'

So Orazio was still a socialist. Not surprising. I wasn't interested in politics tonight though, and I steered the conversation back to the floor plan of the hotel.

'The Ladies Parlor is across the hall?' I asked.

'Yes, you can go see it. I can't join you though. It's for women only.'

'No, that's not necessary.' I didn't ask him if he'd seen Lucia leave the Parlor the night Alessa died. I didn't want to seem obsessed with her death. 'Have we walked a block yet?'

'Almost. A few more steps through the vestibule, and here we are!'

A doorman swung the double doors open wide, and we stepped out on to Seventeenth Street.

'That building across the way,' he said, 'is the National Geographic Society. I have spent many free afternoons there.'

Without the National Geographic Society the OSS wouldn't have maps of half the countries we were fighting in.

'You don't have your wrap, come back inside,' Orazio said. 'It's chilly.'

Once the doorman closed the door behind us, we heard music.

'The Mayflower Orchestra is playing,' Orazio said. 'I do so hope you don't jitterbug.'

I couldn't help but laugh. 'Hardly,' I said, though Madeleine and Ada had tried to teach me. 'The foxtrot and the waltz compose my entire repertoire.'

'Thank God,' he said.

We found our way back through an increasing throng to the Ballroom. The stage rose, and Sidney Seideman, the famous violinist and conductor, climbed up the steps to take his place leading the orchestra. Seideman oversaw several orchestras in Washington, but on a night like this he was expected to be at the Mayflower.

The crowd cheered as he raised his baton, and the band launched into Glenn Miller's 'String of Pearls'. The crowd moved into the middle of the dance floor like an ocean wave rippling on to a beach.

I confess that in the excitement I forgot about Alessa for a time.

'I think we can foxtrot to this,' Orazio said, taking my hand and leading me out on to the floor. We joined couples in glamorous evening dress, sailors, USO hostesses, and military officers in dress uniforms weighed down with chest hardware, moving about the vast room in time to the music. As it died away, Seideman turned to face the audience. After a few words of welcome, he introduced, to deafening applause, the Incomparable Hildegarde, the most famous supper club entertainer in the world.

She was a blonde hazel-eyed Milwaukee beauty, wearing a slinky sequinned gown and the lipstick and nail color Revlon had named for her. Hildegarde didn't waste any time. She took a microphone from Seideman with a white-gloved hand, turned, and began to sing her signature tune, 'Darling, Je Vous Aime Beaucoup'. It was a slow waltz.

Orazio took me into his arms, and we danced with our bodies touching. 'This is very romantic, no?' he asked.

'Yes, it is,' I said, surprised at the warmth I felt rising in my body from the feel of his arms around me. I thought guiltily of Joe, and then dismissed it. Who wouldn't feel wonderful in such a place with practically anyone!

As Hildegarde's voice trailed away, Orazio and I separated and applauded with the rest of the crowd. Through a gap in the crowd I noticed a familiar figure in military dress blues. Colonel Platon Melinsky, my former handler, lounged against the rail of a VIP box. He was holding the hand of an auburn-haired beauty in a flowing dove-gray gown. The beauty was Myrna.

I turned quickly to Orazio. 'I need to go powder my nose,' I said. 'I'll be right back.'

He didn't have time to answer before I bolted out of the ballroom, my heart pounding and a roar of blood sounding in my ears. I headed for the nearest ladies' room, glad I'd worn my sensible black pumps instead of splurging on high heels.

The lavatory was next to the Ladies' Parlor. I burst through the door with intense relief, glad to find an empty stall, where I sat and waited for my pulse to slow.

I'd been worried about seeing someone who knew me, and now the worst had happened.

I must leave the Mayflower, now, before Melinsky spotted me and wanted to know why I was with Orazio Rossi when I'd been warned away from the Oneto household! What a wasted opportunity! I'd been here an hour and already learned new information about the night of Alessa's death.

And I'd miss the chance to search her room: a slim chance, to be sure, but a chance nonetheless. Yes, solving the puzzle of Alessa's death preoccupied me, but it was more important that I look for the name she'd brought back from New York City! The first slow convoy to Casablanca left in just a few days!

I felt myself calm down, and then a thought struck me.

Did Colonel Melinsky know Orazio Rossi? He'd never met him! He'd seen his name in a police report, that's all!

As my handler, one of his job requirements was to stay away from, first, Alessa, and then the Onetos. That was the definition of an operation involving a cut-out. So if Melinsky saw me with Orazio, he would have no idea who he was! The USO benefit ball was a huge event with thousands of people attending; it was feasible I could be an innocent guest of a friend. I wasn't under house arrest. I had to stay far enough away from Melinsky, and Myrna, that I didn't have to introduce them to Rossi. I'd already taken countless risks and told so many lies that what did one more matter?

Relieved that my plan was salvaged, I left the stall to repair my make-up in front of the lavatory's gilded mirror. This was some bathroom. Marble sinks, marble floors, and marble walls. I'd heard somewhere the fixtures were gold-plated.

I saw a second reflection appear in the mirror. Standing nearby was the Dowager Countess Lucia Oneto.

'Why, hello,' she said, 'Mrs...?' Lucia looked youthful in her dusty pink tulle gown. As Orazio said, she liked to show off her jewels.

She wore a long string of fat pearls around her neck, a four-strand wide pearl cuff with a diamond clasp, and diamond and pearl drop earrings.

'I'm Louise Pearlie,' I said, reminding her.

'How nice to see you again, Lucia. What a lovely dress.'

'I'm so glad you and Orazio could make use of Sebastian's tickets,' she said. 'What a shame to waste them. And Orazio has no friends here, few opportunities to go out socially.'

'It was kind of him to ask me,' I said. 'I'm enjoying myself.'

Lucia drew a gold compact and matching lipstick case from her sequinned evening bag and carefully touched up her face, flicking an invisible bit of something off an eyebrow.

I followed her example, but with a plain powder compact and a drugstore lipstick.

'Orazio is a nice boy,' Lucia continued. 'Not as well born as you might think from his education and manners. His father was in trade. I believe Orazio intended to practice law, until the Depression forced his father out of business.'

'How sad for him!'

'Yes. He and Sebastian became great friends at university. I didn't want Sebastian to go, but his father encouraged him. Parents have so little control over who their children associate with at the universities.'

I didn't trust myself to respond to that, since I would give my right arm to go to college. Instead I focused on carefully outlining my lips.

'After my husband died Sebastian took pity on Orazio's financial predicament and engaged him as his private secretary,' Lucia continued. 'To help with managing the estate. I suppose he has done acceptable work. I have no say in estate matters at all. As Dowager Countess I now survive on a pittance.' She snapped her compact shut and turned to me. 'That's a woman's place in the world, I suppose,' she said. 'We have no head for such things. Our purpose is decorative and maternal.'

I had my own ideas about that, but I didn't say so.

The rest room was next door to the Ladies' Parlor, so I took a few seconds to peer inside. Compared to the other assembly rooms of the hotel, it was small, say twenty-five feet by thirty feet. It would easily hold several bridge tables and then some. When Lucia had played here the night of Alessa's death she could have slipped out on the pretext of using the lavatory or getting a drink and had plenty of time to go upstairs to the Oneto apartment. I saw a bank of four elevators just a few steps away from the parlor and the lavatory.

What intrigued me was that Sebastian,

Lucia, and Orazio were all within shouting distance of each other and an elevator bank at the Seventeenth Street end of the massive hotel. Well away from the main lobby and the service areas, where more people gathered. Either one of them could have slipped away and gone upstairs and either forced Alessa to take an overdose of laudanum or, if she was in the coffee shop getting a sandwich, doctored her tonic. But why? I still didn't see that anyone in the Oneto household had a reasonable motive for murder.

And of course, despite Mayflower security, anyone who looked presentable could have entered the hotel, made his or her way to the Oneto apartment, knocked on the door, and been admitted.

I despaired of ever knowing what had happened to Alessa. I wanted to give up and go home.

But then Orazio found me loitering in the vestibule.

'Come, come,' he said, 'you're missing all the movie stars!'

'I'm sorry I took so long,' I said, taking Orazio's arm. 'I was chatting with Lucia in the ladies' room.'

We entered the Ballroom in time to see Hildegarde and Gene Kelley, dressed in a sailor suit, sing 'For Me and My Gal', followed by Mary Martin in a USO uniform crooning Cole Porter's 'My Heart Belongs to Daddy'.

Thousands packed the Ballroom. I worried less about blowing my cover. It should be easy to avoid anyone I knew in this throng. I noticed Joan Adams with her crowd, jitterbugging away, and all we could do was wave at each other. We couldn't have made our way through the mass of dancers to make introductions even if we wanted to.

Speaking of jitterbugging, when the orchestra struck up another fast song Orazio and I looked at each other and burst out laughing.

'This is a good time to eat,' he said.

'I agree! I'm starving.'

The Presidential Restaurant, where I'd had dinner on Tuesday with Orazio, hosted the buffet. A vast banquet table occupied the center of the room. It groaned with gleaming silver chafing dishes, platters, candlesticks, vases of flowers, sterling tableware, and china. Bunting and flags concealed most of the dark paneling and patriotic decorations.

We picked up our plates and silverware and progressed down the table, helping ourselves to lobster mousse with Normandy sauce, broiled filets of beef, sliced guinea hen, asparagus, scalloped tomatoes, rissole potatoes, broiled mushrooms, and sautéed soft-shelled crabs.

When I got to the end of the buffet table I

noticed Enzo standing there, looking un-comfortable in Mayflower livery. His white-gloved hands hung stiffly at his side.

'Hullo, Enzo,' I said. 'What are you doing here?'

'Overtime,' he answered, gesturing over the gleaming tables. 'Watching the silver.'

'Lord knows there's plenty to watch over,' I said.

'Yes,' he answered, 'we will lose a few spoons tonight, but nothing more, I hope.'

By now our plates overflowed.

'Just think,' Orazio said as we found two adjacent chairs where we could sit together, 'in Britain people are eating creamed herring pie and fried bread.'

'Sounds nasty,' I said. 'Do you think it will come to that here?'

'No,' Orazio said. 'America has more resources, but food shortages will get worse. We should enjoy a good meal while we can.'

'Dessert?' Orazio asked, after we emptied our plates.

'I couldn't possibly,' I said.

'Coffee, then?'

'Please.'

A waiter spirited away our plates before Orazio returned, and I felt gloom settle over me. This evening was so stunning, and Alessa had missed sharing it with Sebastian. Would miss the rest of her life – miss return-ing to her beloved Sicily and miss having children. What a waste. I was so sure she hadn't killed herself; why would she deprive herself of her future? Yes, her life as a refugee was challenging and difficult, but Allied forces were poised to take Sicily on the way to Italy; why would she have despaired now?

But if Alessa had been murdered, I was nowhere close to finding out who'd killed her and why. Sebastian, Orazio, and Lucia's alibis leaked like sieves, but their motives were shaky. And as for opportunity, the woman lived in a vast hotel! Wasn't it more likely that an unknown person, who'd simply walked into the Mayflower and up to her apartment, had killed her? Someone who knew about our operation? And wasn't it likely that that person had made off with the information she'd brought back with her? How could I find out though? I didn't even know her brother's name to warn him! Turi was short for Salvatore, but what was his surname? How many Salvatores worked on the New York docks? It was impossible!

If someone had murdered Alessa, he or she would get away scot-free.

I felt a headache coming on, and I wished I could run out of the front door of the hotel, climb into a pumpkin coach, go home, and go back to work on Monday and file index cards with no memory of Alessa or my pathetic foray into espionage.

'My dear,' Orazio said, setting down our

coffees and a piece of coconut pie, 'are those tears?'

'A few,' I said. 'I'm not preoccupied with Alessa's death, Orazio, I just can't help thinking of her.'

'Yes,' he said, 'I understand. Tell me, when we are done here, shall we go up to the apartment and catch our breaths? Get away from the crowd and the noise? After a rest we can return to the dancing if we like.'

'Yes, let's,' I said. Now was my chance to search Alessa's room.

THIRTY-THREE

Orazio turned his key in the lock and opened the apartment door. 'I don't know if anyone else is home,' he said, ushering me inside. 'Lina?' he called out. 'Sebastian?'

There was no answer.

'Make yourself comfortable,' Orazio said. 'I'll make some coffee.' He vanished into the kitchenette.

I sank on to the sofa gratefully. All that dancing, plus dealing with my fears of getting caught, had worn me out. According to the ormolu clock on the mantle, it was past eleven. It felt like two in the morning to me.

Orazio carried a tray into the living room and set it down on the cocktail table. A wonderful coffee odor arose from an odd contraption on the tray, a sort of jar with what looked like a piston fitted into it.

Orazio saw my puzzlement. 'It's a French press,' he said. 'Makes the best coffee in the world. And uses less coffee than one of your percolators.'

He poured coffee into the simple cups that were part of the standard equipment in a

Mayflower kitchenette.

'Lucia finds it so difficult to adapt to such primitive housekeeping,' Orazio said. 'I think that's why she goes out to tea with her friends so much, so she can eat off china and silver.'

'What happened to the Onetos' property?' I asked.

'The houses, the vineyards and orchards, the sulfur mines, they all still belong to Sebastian,' he said. 'He'll repossess them after the war. Now, of course, he has no income from them; they've been appropriated by the Nazis. The estate's capital, which supports them now, was deposited in Switzerland by Sebastian's father. As to the houses themselves, I expect they have been looted.'

'That's too bad,' I said.

Orazio shrugged. 'Lives are more important than possessions. The Sicilian people are desperate.'

'When the Allies occupy the island, life will be better.'

'I hope so.'

I kicked off my shoes, curled my feet up under me on the sofa, and sipped my coffee. To my relief Orazio showed no signs of seducing me. There were women spies working for OSS who were willing to sleep with men to get information, but I wasn't one of them!

Which made me wonder about Myrna.

What was she doing with Colonel Melinsky? The coincidence concerned me. Myrna worked for OSS, or she wouldn't have been at 'The Farm' with me. It was possible that they'd simply met at work. Melinsky could afford tickets to the ball, and Myrna was a gorgeous woman. Why shouldn't he ask her out? I couldn't imagine any other reason they would be at the ball.

I lingered over my coffee as long as I could. Orazio finished his.

'Do you mind?' he asked as he took a cigarette out of a silver box on the cocktail table and held it up.

'Not at all,' I said.

'Would you care for one?'

'No, thanks. Smoking makes my throat sore.'

Orazio lit his cigarette. I decided I had until he finished smoking it to figure out how to search Alessa's room. How to get back into the bedroom area of the apartment? It seemed too obvious to ask to use the bathroom.

'Would you like to powder your nose before we go back downstairs?' Orazio asked, crushing the butt of his cigarette out in an ashtray.

'Yes, thank you, I would,' I said. I couldn't believe my luck. Almost made me believe in Providence.

'If you go through that door,' he began,

gesturing towards the door to the bedroom hallway.

'I know the way,' I said. 'I used Lucia's bathroom at the memorial service.'

Once in the hallway I closed the door and made sure it latched. I was still in my stocking feet to keep from making noise. I opened the door to Lucia's bathroom and closed it. I didn't know what Orazio could hear in the living room, but I wanted to make it sound like I was doing what I was supposed to be doing. On the way back from Alessa's room I'd slip in the bathroom and flush the toilet.

Alessa's and Sebastian's door was open. Inside, the room looked much like it had when I'd seen it on the afternoon of Alessa's memorial reception. It was clear that Sebastian slept alone now. The table next to his side of the bed held a carafe and water tumbler, reading glasses, an open book, and a wadded up handkerchief. Alessa's side table held only a lamp.

It looked as though Sebastian had begun to clean out her things but he hadn't gotten very far. Poor man. I don't suppose his mother was much help to him. It wouldn't be easy for Lina, either.

Alessa's closet door was open, revealing her clothes. I noticed a Saks garment bag hanging inside. Her ball gown for tonight. I felt tears begin to form and ruthlessly suppressed them. Alessa was dead. I doubted I would ever know how or why.

My job now was to try to find the letter I hoped she had brought back from New York.

Her knitting bag still sat on the floor under the desk.

It couldn't be that simple, could it? Quickly and quietly I pulled the bag out from under the desk and riffled through it. I found a skein of wool, several pairs of knitting needles, and an almost completed pair of fingerless gloves.

In a side pocket where Alessa kept her patterns I discovered a small, stiff rectangle. I felt almost light-headed as I pulled an envelope identical to the two previous ones Alessa had given me from her bag.

This was it. I'd found it. Alessa's death hadn't been in vain!

For second I was overwhelmed. Then I realized I had to get back to the living room and Orazio before he became suspicious.

I stuffed the envelope into the bodice of my dress and got to my feet, turning to the door.

Orazio stood there, leaning against the door jamb, with a revolver in his hand.

THIRTY-FOUR

I stared at Orazio's revolver.

'Like it?' he said. 'It's an old Beretta. Custom made, leather grip, engraved. Sebastian's, of course.'

I pulled myself together and concocted a lie as quickly as I could. 'What on earth are you doing with that?' I asked. 'I know I'm snooping, but a gun is hardly necessary. I surrender, OK?

'I knew you'd lead me to it,' he said. 'I didn't dare search myself, and I had no idea where to look. Her knitting bag – I should have realized!'

'I don't know what you're talking about,' I said. 'I apologize for coming in here – it's inexcusable, I know – but I saw the open door, and I wanted something to remember Alessa by. It's a knitting pattern she wrote out.'

'Don't insult me,' Orazio said. 'That's a letter from Alessa's bastard brother. Her bastard *Mafioso capodecina* brother. With information for the OSS. I want it. Give it to me.'

So Turi was Alessa's asset!

'No,' I said, stupidly determined. 'It's none of your business.'

Orazio pointed the gun directly at me.

'You can't shoot me; someone will hear the gunshot,' I said. 'How would you explain?'

Orazio laughed. 'All the apartments nearby are empty. The rich people who live in them are downstairs at the ball. And the hotel is solidly built, a shining example of capitalism.'

'Orazio,' I said, 'I don't know what concern this is of yours, but I promise you that this letter contains information that's critical to the war effort.'

'I have my sources, too. I'm a member of the Italian Communist Party. We have spies of our own on the New York City docks. We know the Mafia is working for the United States government.'

'You followed Alessa to her last meeting with Turi!'

'No. How stupid would that be? She might have recognized me. It was one of our agents.'

'The Mafia is keeping the New York docks safe from Nazi espionage. How can you object to that?'

'The Mafia does nothing without compensation! Luciano and his fellow criminals will expect a reward after the war. What do you think it could be? Could it be Sicily?'

'That's not important now. We have to win

first.'

'It's important to me! The only good thing Mussolini did was expel the Mafia! If those hoodlums return to Sicily after the war, the Sicilian people will be back under the thumbs of criminals – when they're not working themselves to death for people like Sebastian in his olive groves and his sulfur mines! The only chance we have to be free is if the Mafia stays out of Sicily forever!'

Orazio was so angry he trembled.

'And for someone like me...' he said. 'I'll have to work for someone like Sebastian for the rest of my life. I despise him! He's useless for anything but reading poetry. But rich nonetheless! And his mother, my God, what a harpy. She bribed me with a diamond bracelet to tell me the contents of Sebastian's will!

Orazio drew back his fist and slammed it into a wall mirror next to the door. It splintered into tiny pieces, showering his shoulders with shards of glass. I found myself crouched behind Alessa's armoire.

Orazio was angry enough to commit murder, I could see that. And he'd had the opportunity to doctor Alessa's tonic, while Alessa was at the coffee shop eating her sandwich. He must have killed her to keep her from giving me the name of the Mafia sleeper she'd brought back from New York.

I kept my mouth shut. Orazio must not

know I suspected him or I'd never leave this apartment alive. I didn't see that I had any choice but to give Orazio what he wanted. But still I hesitated.

'Give it to me, and I'll let you go,' he said. 'I swear. You'll tell your masters that your operation failed. That will be the end of it.' Some of the anger faded from his face. He lowered the gun slightly.

I tried to reason with him. 'This one bit of information won't seal Sicily's fate,' I said. 'But it will protect countless convoys and lives. You want the Allies to invade Sicily to free it, don't you?'

Anger built up in him again. I could see his shoulders shake.

'Give it to me,' he said, 'or I will shoot you. I will.'

I believed him. I drew the envelope from my bodice and handed it over to him.

'At last!' He tucked it into his pocket. 'Now,' he said, waving the pistol, 'let's go.'

'Go where?'

'You didn't believe me when I said I'd let you go, did you? Stupid woman.' He grabbed me with his left hand, pulled me to him, so that his face was close to mine, the gun at my head. 'We're going to the sub-basement,' he said. 'No one will be there to help you.'

I admit it, I was terrified. Orazio was taller, heavier, and stronger than me. And he had a gun.

Size and strength have nothing to do with defending yourself. Everything Sergeant Smith had taught me at 'The Farm' returned to me in one instinctive fluid movement. I rammed Orazio in the face with the flat of my left hand, digging my fingers deep into his eyes. I could feel the jelly of his eyeballs under my nails.

Orazio screamed in agony. He flung his right hand, holding the gun, wide. When he fell to the floor I crouched over him and kneed him as hard as I could in the scrotum. He screamed again and doubled over into a fetal position, clutching his groin. Blood trickled from one eye.

I dropped to the floor next to him and dug into his jacket pocket and found Alessa's letter. I clutched it with bloody fingers and headed for the bedroom door.

But I was an amateur still, and I forgot to pick up the gun! Orazio pulled himself to a sitting position, grabbed the gun, and fired at my back. A bullet splintered the door jamb next to my head as I almost fell into the hall.

The next bullet will kill me, I thought. It's all over. I turned to face Orazio.

I heard the gunshot and saw the gun barrel flash, but in that split second Enzo came out of nowhere and dived between Orazio and me. His squat body jerked from the impact of the bullet, and he dropped to the floor like a stone.

I had enough time in the few seconds before Orazio realized Enzo wasn't me to dig into my handbag, flick open my knife, and rush at Orazio. Orazio didn't expect me to attack him, and by sheer luck I reached him and stabbed him in the ribs while he wiped blood from his eyes. Orazio crashed to the floor again, moaning.

I crushed his right hand with the heel of my shoe and ripped the gun from his hand. He screamed again. I stuffed Alessa's letter back into my dress bodice and drew my bloody knife out of Orazio's ribs. Withdrawing the knife made a grating sound that sent a shiver down my spine.

I didn't care how empty this hotel floor was; someone must have heard all this commotion. I had to get out of that apartment.

Enzo lay bleeding in the hallway, a hand clutched to his shoulder. I didn't stop to ask him how or why he'd known to come to my rescue.

I grabbed him by his good arm, ducked under it, and dragged him to his feet and into the bathroom. I folded a bright white towel over his wound, bound it with one of Lucia's nylons hanging over a towel bar, and forced him to his feet.

'We have to get out of here.'

'You go,' Enzo said. 'I can't make it.'

'We don't have to go far,' I said. 'Just to the

elevator and down a couple of floors.'

The hall was empty, but I could hear excited voices in the apartment across the way. It wouldn't be long before Mayflower Hotel security would arrive.

The elevator was empty. I punched the button for two floors below.

Enzo leaned heavily on me, blood seeping through the makeshift bandage I'd bound to his shoulder.

'You saved my life,' I said to Enzo. 'Thank you.'

'It was my duty,' he said. As the elevator door opened Enzo slumped.

'Walk, damn it!' I said. 'It's just a few steps!'

Enzo struggled down the short hall to Joan Adams' apartment. I knew she hid a key behind her name card on the door.

In seconds I was inside and the door was locked again.

I figured Joan would still be at the ball, but instead she rose from the sofa, dressed in a silk dressing gown.

'What the hell!' she said. 'Louise!'

'Please don't ask questions,' I said. 'Trust me! We need help!'

'So I see,' she said. 'Let's get your friend into the bathroom before he bleeds all over the carpet.'

We sat Enzo on the toilet and removed the blood soaked towel. We peeled off his coat and shirt. Joan examined his back.

'There's no exit wound,' she said. 'That's bad. He needs a doctor quickly.'

Joan owned a surprising cache of first-aid supplies. Enzo groaned and flinched in pain as we cleaned his wound with iodine and dressed it with a thick gauze pad secured with a strip of towel.

Enzo's livery tunic and undershirt were stained with blood. So was my new, beautiful ball gown.

'We need to get out of the hotel,' I said.

'I can lend you a coat. As for your friend, I'm a big girl. I might be able to find a shirt he could wear. Is security looking for you? Have the police been called?'

'I don't know,' I said. Orazio must have summoned help. What he would tell the help when it arrived I couldn't imagine.

'Joan,' I said, 'you're not asking me any questions.'

'Would you answer them?'

'Probably not.'

'OK then.'

'*Signoras*,' Enzo said, wincing with pain. 'You must not endanger yourselves to help me. Take me to the service elevator. I will go the sub-basement and attempt to escape that way. If I am arrested I will confess to everything. *Signora* Pearlie, cover yourself with your friend's coat and go to the lobby and get a cab.'

'No,' I said. 'You saved my life. We're both getting out of here.'

A knock sounded at Joan's door.

'I'd better answer that,' she said.

I heard her talking to two men but couldn't hear the conversation clearly.

Joan's front door closed, and she came back into the bathroom. 'Let's get you to the sofa,' she said to Enzo. 'You'll be more comfortable.'

We helped him lie down and cushioned his head with one of Joan's silk pillows.

'That was a Mayflower security guard and a DC policeman,' Joan said. 'Orazio Rossi told them that you, Louise, attempted to steal Alessa Oneto's jewelry. Enzo was your accomplice, supposedly.'

'That pig!' I said.

'Surely this can be cleared up?'

'Joan,' I said, 'I can't be arrested and searched right now.'

She raised an eyebrow at me.

'I have a Top Secret document in my possession.'

'What will we do?' Enzo said. 'The police will be all over the hotel by now.'

'I know.' I turned to Joan. 'I could leave the document with you, and Enzo and I could surrender to the police. We can make up our own story, and it would be our word against Rossi's.'

'That is good,' Enzo said, sitting up, and

310

wincing. 'We could say that Rossi was attempting to take advantage of you, that I heard your screams as I passed by on an errand!'

'That's quite a tale,' Joan said. 'I can see the front page of *The Washington Post* now. Reporters will be everywhere, questioning everyone. Who knows what could come out? What Sebastian and Lucia might say? Our employer would be furious.'

I stared at Joan. 'You know all about this, don't you!'

'About what? I need to make a phone call.' She dialed the hotel operator. 'I need you to deliver a message to the man sitting on the banquette to the left of the door to the coffee shop. He's wearing a chauffeur's uniform,' she said into the receiver.

'What are you doing?' I asked.

'Calling the cavalry. Would either of you like a glass of water? Or maybe something stronger?'

I requested water, while Enzo accepted a shot glass of bourbon, tossing it back in one gulp.

'By the way,' I said to him. 'How did you happen to be outside the Oneto apartment door?'

'I was watching you,' he said. 'When I saw you at the ball with Rossi, I knew you must still be questioning Countess Alessa's death. I determined to follow you. Rossi had left the door of the apartment unlocked. When I heard the sounds of your dispute, I rushed inside.'

'But why did you decide to protect me?'

'Honor,' he said, shrugging. 'Tradition. I failed to see that Countess Alessa was in danger. I didn't want anything to happen to you.'

I rounded on Joan. 'You were watching me, too!'

'I admit I was. I had instructions to keep you under surveillance. When I saw you leave the ball with Rossi I thought the best thing for me to do was to come to my apartment in case you needed me.'

'Who instructed you to watch me, and why? I don't understand.'

A soft knock sounded at the door. Joan opened the door. Colonel Melinsky and Myrna slipped inside.

I stared open-mouthed at them as the truth dawned. It wasn't a coincidence that they were at the Mayflower together tonight. I remembered that Betty told me Myrna had found a new apartment. Of course! OSS had set her up at the Mayflower Hotel as an agent! Tonight she had joined Melinsky as his 'date' to watch me!

'How could you!' I said, furious. 'You set me up!'

'We thought it would be best this way,' Melinsky said.

'What way?' I said. 'Why? How did you know I was even going to be here tonight!'

'You know he can't tell you. Hush and listen,' Myrna said.

'No time,' Melinsky said. 'We need to get Louise and – who are you?' he asked Enzo.

'Enzo Carini,' Enzo said. 'I work in the silver room. I followed when *Signora* Pearlie went upstairs with *Signore* Rossi.'

'He saved my life, no thanks to you,' I said. I was so angry that I forgot to tell him I had Alessa's information.

'Come, I will explain,' Melinsky said. 'We must get the two of you out of the hotel.'

'What about Rossi and his story?' I asked.

'We will take care of Mr Orazio Rossi,' Melinsky said.

'He killed Alessa. To keep her from delivering the take to us. Did you know?'

'No,' Melinsky said. 'We suspected Alessa was murdered. But we weren't sure by whom or why.'

'Joan and I need to get Enzo to a hospital,' Myrna said. 'He's still bleeding.'

'We need to get you away from here, too,' Melinsky said to me.

Joan fetched a black cloak from her wardrobe and threw it over my shoulders. Melinsky took me by the arm and led me out into the hall to the stairs.

'Down to the second floor,' he said, quietly. 'We have been watching Rossi,' he continued, almost whispering. 'He is a member of a radical group, communists, that intend to seize the government of Sicily as soon as the island is liberated. When Alessa contacted you, we were afraid that Rossi would discover her plan and threaten the alliance between the Mafia and the Office of Naval Intelligence.'

I stopped on the landing. 'You...' I didn't dare call him the names I wanted!. 'You kept me in the dark! You knew Alessa had been murdered! You faked my suspension! You let me think my job was in jeopardy!'

'Keep moving, please,' he said.

I stood my ground. 'You meant for me to keep trying to solve Alessa's murder and find the information she brought from New York, without backup! I was out there naked!'

'Yes, yes,' he said, almost dragging me down the steps to the Seventeenth Street lobby and then out into the street.

Jack waited for me there, holding open the door of a decent car for once, a maroon Cadillac LaSalle.

'We judged that the operation would go best if you were ignorant of most of the details,' he said. 'That way whatever you did would look, well, personal.'

And if I got in trouble OSS wouldn't be involved!

Melinsky hadn't trusted my competence enough to brief me completely. During the entire operation he knew Rossi was dangerous, that he might find out what Alessa was doing, but he'd never told me. Would Alessa still be alive if she'd been warned about Rossi? I'd never know.

What I did know, however, was that it was in my best interest not to say anything. But I could think what I wanted – and I thought Platon Melinsky and all the other men at OSS who'd deceived me were louses.

'Louise,' Melinsky said, 'please understand. The information Alessa had was more important than her life. I'm so sorry we never found it, but this is wartime. Sacrifices must be made.'

I reached into my bodice and pulled out Alessa's missive and jammed it into his hand.

'You got it!' Melinsky said. 'Why didn't you say so!'

Again I bit my tongue, but I couldn't contain one comment.

'The blood had better come out of this dress!' I said.

EPILOG

Hell's Kitchen Park was dank and dark at midnight. A cold wind swayed the bare branches of nearby trees, and their susurration muffled the noise of the traffic on Amsterdam Avenue. I'd armed myself with a hooded flashlight, my knife – wiped clean of Orazio Rossi's blood – and a police whistle.

I glanced at my watch. Turi was late.

I'd been so lucky to find him. It occurred to me that if Alessa had used the false last name di Luca in honor of her father, that Turi might have used it, too, as his bastard son. Sure enough the New York dockworkers' union rolls listed one Salvatore di Luca, a winch operator assigned to Pier 84.

He slid on to the bench next to me. I saw little of Alessa in him. He was stocky and muscular, with jet-black hair, black eyes, where Alessa's were blue, and large hands with thick fingers.

'Thank you for coming,' I said.

Turi shook his head. 'It is I who must thank you. I saw in the newspapers that my sister had died, but I never believed it was suicide. And I'd assumed our mission was a failure. Until a few days ago.'

'When the "sleeper" was arrested?'

'Yes, and when no one came to kill me afterwards. My children still have a father. Can you tell me what happened to Alessa?'

'She was murdered by Orazio Rossi, her husband's private secretary. He was a member of the Italian Communist Party in exile. He found out from—'

Turi raised his hand. 'Don't tell me,' he said. 'It is best I don't know. There are so many spies on the docks. Nazis, and even Reds. One of them must have followed me to my meetings with Alessa. And I was so careful! I so badly wanted to deliver my *capo* to American intelligence in a way that would not get me killed. Instead Alessa died.'

Turi broke down, burying his head in his hairy hands, sobbing softly until tears trickled through his fingers.

I wept, too, with a hand on his shoulder.

Turi lifted his head, pulling a bandanna out of a pocket and wiping his face. 'So,' he said, 'what will happen to Rossi?'

I hated to tell him this. 'OSS has swept the entire incident under the carpet. Alessa's death is still listed as a suicide.'

Turi turned to me, incredulous. 'No!' he said.

'Rossi is on his way to England. As soon as Sicily is liberated he will return there to spy on the communists in return for his freedom.' Just saying those words made me angry. I couldn't fault OSS for recruiting Rossi. He could prove to be a valuable double agent. But the injustice of it rankled. I'd blinded Rossi in one eye when we fought in Alessa's bedroom, but that was a small price for him to pay for her murder.

'What ship did he take?' Turi asked.

'To England?' I said, surprised. 'I don't know. But I can find out.'

'Send me a telegram as soon as you learn it. I know many Mafia *soldati* in the merchant marine union. Rossi will, sadly, drink too much in the saloon and fall overboard before his ship docks in London.'

AFTERWORD

In 1946, as a reward for his wartime co-operation, Mafia boss 'Lucky' Luciano was paroled on condition that he leave the United States and return to Sicily. He died at Naples International Airport in 1962 of a heart attack, but was buried in Queens. Two thousand people attended his funeral.